BOBBY WAYNE FICTION PRESENTS

THE
FEATRAL
THE ADVANCEMENT OF WARFARE

A SCIENCE FICTION NOVEL

I0553119

BOBBY WAYNE

Bobby Wayne Fiction

The Featral
The Advancement of Warfare

Author: Bobby Wayne
Published by: Bobby Wayne Fiction
www.bobbywaynefiction.com
Copyright © 2021 by Bobby Wayne
Copyright © 2013 Registration Number TXu-1-895-610
ISBN 979-8-9853475-2-4 (Paperback)
ISBN 979-8-9853475-3-1 (eBook)

This book was printed in the United States of America.

contents

THE BEGINNING

IT STARTED SMALLER than a grain of salt...
That's the size of a cell formed on the first day after the sperm joins with the ovum. At that moment, twenty-three chromosomes from each parent join to create every detail of human development: sex, eye color, demeanor, skin tone, hair, height, personality, emotion, and many other inherited characteristics.

By day four the egg rapidly divides. It makes its way down the fallopian tube into the uterus. The uterus prepares itself for the fertilized egg.

Within two weeks, the zygote implants in the lining of the uterus. It splits into two distinct sets of cells. Half becomes the placenta, which provides nourishment for the fetus, and the other half becomes the fetus itself.

At week three, the placenta and umbilical cord are fully functional. The foundations for the brain, spinal cord, and nervous system are established. The heart beats.

When one month has passed, the backbone and muscles form. Hair sprouts, and eyes, ears, arms, and legs show.

At week six the embryo is 10,000 times larger than the original fertilized egg. The heart pumps increasing quantities of blood through the circulatory system. Five fingers can be discerned on each hand. The eyes darken as pigment is produced. The liver takes over the production of blood cells. Brain waves can be detected and recorded. The brain controls the movement of muscles and organs.

At week seven the embryo is in continuous movement. The jaw forms, including teeth. The eyelids seal to protect the embryo's developing and sensitive eyes.

At two months, the fetus has everything found in a fully developed adult. The stomach produces digestive juices. The kidneys operate. Genitals form. Forty muscle sets work in conjunction with the nervous system. The fetus responds to touch.

At week nine the fetus can curve its fingers around an object in its palm. Fingerprints are evident in the skin. Fingernails and hair develop and grow.

By week twelve the fetus can bend, stretch, open its hands, make a fist, squint, lift its head, swallow, and wrinkle its forehead. The fetus breathes amniotic fluid. It sleeps, awakens, exercises, turns its head, curls its toes, and opens and closes its mouth.

Week thirteen to week sixteen: This is the only time the government sponsored and paid for abortions— not a day earlier or a day later. No one at the time knew why.

The date was September 6, 2089…

THE DECISION

LOS ANGELES. THE sun shone brightly, even though it was still early. It was a hot and humid morning that promised an even more brutal afternoon. The boundaries of the seasons had become more extreme over the past decade. Summers were unbearable, as were the winters. One didn't want to be outside for long. In fact, it was hazardous to do so.

But those flying their vehicles within the 405-freeway grid cruised comfortably within their crafts of various makes and models. This was the case with a young teenage girl who was flying on the grid that morning.

Traffic was light. The grid allowed flight travel, in an orderly fashion, at differing heights within the grid's parameters. Craft communicated with each other for spacing and direction. Within the grid, traffic accidents had virtually been eliminated.

The young teen directed her vehicle, a Ford Hawk, to exit and connect with another street grid. During the transition, she pondered what it had been like when people drove cars on roads. She had always appreciated the safety the grid provided as well as the comforts afforded by the modern crafts. But safety and comfort were not her concern now. She was uneasy. She needed to reach her journey's end.

Other airborne craft flashed by to the left of her in the opposite direction. As she neared her destination, a voice from the vehicle's guidance system gave her instructions. "Your destination is to the right. Please prepare to convert to manual control to exit the grid."

She looked over at a large building coming into view. "Exit grid, convert to manual control," the teen commanded. She felt the control of the craft return to her. She turned the craft and glided it toward the building and into an open parking area. The sun's reflection glistened brightly off the parked vehicles below. She continued to glide around searching for a space as the parking lot was noticeably crowded.

Most similarly sized lots had guidance systems that would communicate with vehicles and monitor pedestrian traffic. Noting an opening, she directed her vehicle over to the space. At her command, the vehicle hovered gently into the space and powered down.

She took a deep breath and then paused to gaze out of her tinted window toward the building in front of her. It was the government clinic. The teen sat for a few moments to pull herself together.

She was only seventeen years old, much too young to be concerned about the complexities of life. She was normally a very confident and decisive person. She had been the regional martial arts champion for her school and was used to a sense of control and respect in her life. However, none of that would help her here. She had made a mistake, and it had to be fixed.

The teen twisted her finger through her brown stringy hair, twirling the lock out of nervous habit. Then she looked up at the mirror. Even though her complexion had a golden tone to it, she looked paler than usual. The eyes returning her glare revealed inner turmoil and a lack of sleep. With a twinge of anxiety, she gently placed her hand on her stomach. She was having second thoughts.

The alarm from her watch triggered a holographic image. The image was of herself who appeared seated in the passenger's seat next to her. "Everything is OK," the image said. "Everything is safe. It's a government clinic. In a few hours, this will be done with, and you can get back to your life."

Yes. In a few hours, this will be over with.

"Be strong," the image continued. "Just get out of the car and go inside. They'll take care of you. There is nothing to worry about. Laura did this twice and said it was no big deal. They put you to sleep now, so you won't feel a thing. You wake up, and it's over." The image paused, waiting for the girl to move. "Just get inside out of the heat," it said. Then it disappeared.

The teen commanded the vehicle to maintain its inside temperature. "Sixty-five degrees." She took another deep breath, then grabbed her purse and got out.

The oppressively hot air hit her immediately. When she blinked, she could feel the coolness in her eyes in comparison with the atmosphere around her. She wasted no time, walking rapidly toward the doors of the clinic.

It was only a short walk, but perspiration began to form on her body even before she made it to the front of the building. Several other women were also approaching the clinic doors. The doors automatically slid open for them to enter and then slid shut behind them.

"God, it's hot today," a middle-aged woman said, gesturing with her hand. "Well, I guess it's always hot this time of year, isn't it?" The woman spoke casually as if they were simply walking into a grocery store. She didn't appear to be at all nervous about what they were about to do.

The young teen acknowledged her as they proceeded inside and approached a line that was forming.

"Whew, but it feels good in here," the woman said. "Is this your first time?"

"Yes," the young teen replied, nodding.

"Don't worry about a thing. You're not alone. They'll explain everything and answer all of your questions," the woman said as they got into line behind several other women. "This is my fourth time at this clinic. They treat you good here. Just relax."

The teen forced an uneasy nod.

Their attention was suddenly drawn to a low humming sound. They looked up and saw a seven-foot-tall armed security robot. It resembled an armored man. It was not an uncommon sight, as such robots made up much of society's security force. It stood perfectly still except for the occasional turning of its head back and forth.

The teen turned away from the robot and glanced at the large seating area. She was taken aback at the great number of patients who were already seated there. A small number of men, parents, and friends were also seated next to some patients for support. But the teen was alone. She was by herself.

She returned her focus on the line in front of her. A plain looking nurse was sitting behind a large counter. In front of the nurse was an opened three-sided plexiglass enclosure, which allowed patients to step up between its walls. Inside the enclosure was a hand scanner that downloaded and registered the patients' information. The nurse had a floating screen in front of her that downloaded patient data.

The teen watched as a young woman stepped inside the plexiglass enclosure. The woman responded to the machine's command to place her right hand on the hand-shaped scanner. After it registered her information, other scanners within the enclosure's walls took an inventory of her body.

Suddenly, the security robot turned its head and looked at the woman within the plexiglass. The nurse glared at the woman in a condescending manner.

"Ms. Croner, you were here three weeks ago. It's still too early. You were told to come back after September fourteenth."

"But I know it's a girl. Why can't you just do it now?" the woman asked.

"The sex does not matter in the jurisdiction of the States. You do not get special consideration here."

"But I need to get it out of me. I don't want to be pregnant. Aren't I close enough for you? What do you care?"

"You know the rules, Ms. Croner. There are no exceptions. You certainly can go to a private clinic and have the procedure done ahead of time if you wish.

However, you do so at your own risk and expense. Otherwise, please come back after the fourteenth."

"Nobody can afford to do that," the woman scoffed. "What's the big deal about thirteen weeks anyway? It doesn't make sense to me."

"The government has determined it's the safest time. Again, there are no exceptions. Please come after the fourteenth."

Ms. Croner looked up at the large robot, which had stepped up closer to her. She turned away, mumbling under her breath, then stormed out of the enclosure toward the exit.

The robot's gaze followed her until she left the building. Then it resumed its previous position.

The middle-aged woman who had come in the door with the young teen patted her on the back. "The nerve of some people, huh?" she whispered.

Just then, the nurse behind the counter waved for the young teen to step forward. "Some women just don't want to obey the rules. Come on, honey. It's alright."

The teen stepped inside the enclosure and placed her hand on the scanner in response to the machine's command. She remained still while the machine read the condition of her body. As was the case with everyone in society, the chip in her hand provided access to all sorts of information about her: her identity, medical records, genealogy, her voice recognition ID, and her bank account, although the phrase "bank account" was now redundant. All financial transactions were applied directly to and from the chip.

"You're fine," the nurse replied. "You're fourteen and a half weeks. Would you like to talk to a counselor today?"

The teen shook her head. The nurse returned an understanding smile. "Take a seat. We'll call you."

As she said this, the scanner produced a receipt with a number on it. The teen thought it ironic that a government operation would still use paper receipts.

"Make sure you watch the presentation. You'll be prompted with a choice to talk to a counselor if you change your mind."

The teen thanked the nurse and then looked at the number in her hand: 237.

Despite the number of people inside, finding a seat was not a problem. She found one away from everyone else's personal space. She sat with her purse in her lap. After several seconds, a three-dimensional holographic screen appeared in front of her. Earphones were produced from the arm of the chair. With some hesitation, she reached for the earphones. When she put them on, the presentation commenced.

The image of a pleasant-looking, middle-aged, fit Caucasian woman appeared. The woman was designed to look like the teen, except older. She wore a tailored navy-blue dress. Her brown hair was neatly pinned, and her nails polished. She appeared confident but with the gentleness of a caring mother. Her makeup was perfectly applied. Her voice was that of comfort. The image smiled as it spoke in a gentle voice. "Welcome, citizen. It is understandable that some women may have misgivings about ending their pregnancy. You may be one of these women. However, this procedure is a natural concept that advances harmony in society.

We're committed to your safety, and we desire to make your experience as pleasant as possible."

At that moment, the middle-aged woman whom the teen had come in with plopped down next to her. The teen could tell she wanted to engage in small talk.

"Numbers one twenty-one to one forty please report to sector A," a voice announced over the intercom.

"Pause," the teen said, stopping the presentation to acknowledge the woman.

"They take us in twenty at a time," the woman explained. "They have around forty rooms back there, you know." While she was still speaking, the woman's chair produced earphones and a holographic image to begin a presentation. "Screen off," the woman said. The image disappeared.

"Does it hurt?" the young teen asked.

"You're out the whole time. So, you don't feel anything. I mean, you're a little sore down there afterward, for like a day or so, but they give you medication for that. You can talk to a counselor if you want."

"No, I'm OK with this. I can't afford to deal with a kid at this time of my life. It has to be done."

The woman nodded gently in understanding, then sat back and left the teen alone to resume her presentation.

"Reactivate presentation," the girl commanded.

The holographic woman reappeared with her hands gently folded together. She smiled lovingly at the young teen. In fact, she never stopped smiling, which brought an unrealistic quality to the image. "I am here to put your mind at ease and answer any questions you might have," the image said. "I can answer your questions regarding the process, this facility, and the benefits of your decision to the global community. Dear citizen, how would you like to proceed?"

For several long seconds, the young teen sat there deep in thought. The image smiled back at her, waiting for her reply. "Dear citizen, how would you like to proceed?"

The teen continued to look at the image. Finally, she asked the question that had been bothering her for days. "Does it have a soul?"

For several seconds the image didn't respond or move. "I do not understand. Please rephrase your question."

"Does it have a soul?"

Another long pause.

"I do not understand. Please rephrase your question."

The young teen rolled her eyes. "You're the one who doesn't have a soul," she said under her breath. "Recovery time then. How soon will it be until I can return to my normal school activities?"

"Thank you for your question. You will be pleased to know most women can return to normal activities the following day." The image continued to talk about activities and then subsequently responded to the teen's follow-up questions. She sat through the rest of the interactive presentation with one ear listening and the other in anticipation of her number being called.

When the numbers were called out, patients made their way, twenty at a time, to their sectors. The calls had been averaging around fifteen minutes apart. She sat and waited. The other woman didn't bother her, instead reading for pleasure on her CronePad reading device.

After a while, the young teen had enough of listening to the holographic lady and her artificial reassurances. They had already called up to number 220. She would be in the next batch. She placed her purse in her lap, closed her eyes, and waited.

It had happened not long ago, the moment still fresh in her mind. It was just a little party. Just a few kids having some fun and enjoying some alcohol and music. Most of the kids she already knew. There were no drugs around, and it didn't seem like a big deal. She simmered with regret knowing she wasn't even going to go at first. Her friends had talked her into it. Something kept telling her to leave, but she didn't. Then it happened—he happened. A few moments of inebriated pleasure, and it was over. The sad part was she didn't even like the guy. *Why do I have to suffer the consequences of this and not him?*

Twenty minutes more passed. It seemed like an eternity. Finally, the voice sounded again. "Numbers two hundred and twenty-one to two forty please report to sector C."

"That's us," the woman next to her said. They both gathered their belongings and proceeded to sector C.

As with the other sectors, sector C had two wide doors with robotic guards posted on both sides. When they had all gathered, the doors slid open. A nurse appeared and asked the patients to hold their right hand over the scanner as they entered, one by one.

The young teen didn't understand why there was so much security and precautions. However, it did make her feel safe.

During this time, another nurse gave them instructions. Once inside, they were to strip naked and place their belongings in the locker that corresponded to their number. Then they were to proceed through another door designated for sanitation. After sanitation, they were to come back, put on the robe provided, and proceed to the corresponding gurney. In case they didn't remember the instructions, they would be repeated every few minutes.

Once inside, the teen walked up and faced her cabinet-style locker. It had chest height partitions separating the women and giving them a small sense of modesty. It had a cushioned chair in front of it. The number above read "237," and her name was displayed beneath. She looked over and acknowledged the woman she had come in with. The teen gave her a nervous smile, and the woman smiled in return.

The teen took off her clothes, being somewhat self-conscious that cameras were in view. She secured her belongings, put on the light robe provided and then proceeded to the sanitation room. A hair covering was made available, of which most women took advantage. The teen decided to pass on it. She waited her turn until the narrow enclosure opened to beckon her inside. It was made of glass with small armrests that automatically adjusted to her height. As she stepped inside, the door slid closed behind her.

"Please disrobe and place your robe in the container." A drawer opened on the side. She removed her robe and placed it inside. The drawer closed shut. "Please place your arms on the armrests and your feet onto the diagram on the floor."

She did so.

"For your safety, please remain still, and close your eyes during the sanitation process. The process will take approximately twenty seconds."

When she had positioned herself, she closed her eyes. A rush of warm liquid jettisoned onto her body. She flinched at the unexpected pressure. This was followed by water, then a concentrated mist. Finally, she felt the rapid blowing of the air dryers. Then the door and the drawer opened.

"Sanitation is complete. Please put on your robe, return to the locker area, and proceed to the gurney with your designated number."

She was amazed. The sanitation processor was much more thorough and efficient than what she had at home. Her body felt refreshed and clean. She proceeded to the gurneys up against the wall opposite of the lockers. All the gurneys were propped up at forty-five-degree angles. Each was equipped with readers to confirm that the patient matched the gurney. She found her way onto her gurney and sat.

"Please place your right hand on the arm space for scanner reading and IV placement," a voice said. "Once you do, please do not move until completed."

When she placed her hand, a small box arose. The computer immediately confirmed who she was and sized up her vein. Then it inserted the needle and strapped on the adhesive, all in a matter of seconds. She barely had time to flinch.

"Thank you, citizen. You may remove your hand."

The teen laid back and pulled the sheet up for a sense of security.

Nurses came and took the patients out five at a time. She waited her turn. Finally, a Caucasian nurse came to her. The nurse's blond hair was fixed in a bun on top of her head, and she was wearing a loose white outfit. "Are you doing OK?"

"Yes. Thank you."

The nurse pushed her out into a long hallway. It was brightly lit with white floors and walls. "We're going to take you into a room, give you some oxygen and anesthesia, and put you to sleep," the nurse said. "Is that OK with you?"

The teen nodded.

They stopped and turned into one of the rooms with an open door. "Here we go," the nurse said as they entered. Once inside, she positioned the teen's gurney against the wall, then connected the narrow plastic tube protruding from a machine into the teen's IV. The nurse pressed a button, and stirrups appeared from the sides of the gurney. She directed the young teen to place her legs in them, which she did. The nurse patted her on the shoulder and smiled. "The doctor will be with you in a moment." She continued to smile as she left the room.

The room was relatively small, the gurney taking up a good portion of it. There was also a desk and a rolling chair. Protruding from the wall was an apparatus with an oxygen mask.

The several minutes of waiting was excruciating. It was too much time for her to ponder her thoughts. This was especially true with her legs positioned in stirrups. Her eyes began to water. *Maybe I can tell them this was all a mistake. I should have talked to a counselor.*

About this time, a female doctor came in. She placed her hand on the teen's shoulder. "How are you doing?"

"I'm a little nervous," she said, her voice trembling.

"That's understandable, but I assure you there's nothing to be afraid of. In a few minutes, you'll be totally asleep. Then you'll wake up in the recovery room feeling perfectly fine. After an hour or so, you'll be released to go home, with some standard medications. Believe me, we have come a long way in the last hundred years. Would you like to receive counseling?"

The teen closed her eyes to repress her thoughts. When she opened them again her expression became serious. She lost the tremble in her voice and replaced it with one of determination. "No, I have decided. I control my life." The teen looked straight ahead with a cold stare. "I'm ready. It's settled. Let's do this."

"Great!" the doctor replied. "You're making the right decision." The doctor consulted the holographic computer to confirm the teen's data and the images of her uterus. "Alright, I'm going to put the oxygen mask on you now."

The teen nodded in response. The doctor placed the mask on her. Unbeknownst to the young teen, the doctor had already started the anesthesia drug into her IV. The effect was immediate.

"You should be getting drowsy soon," the doctor said.

Her eyes indeed became heavy. She attempted to respond verbally but could not. Her whole body was relaxed. Whatever doubts she had before didn't matter now. She began to lose conscientiousness.

However, in her semiconscious state, she heard foreign sounds she could not identify. She also heard a voice, but it was not the voice of the doctor. It was another voice, and it proclaimed the target was ready.

＊———◆———＊

The hydraulic shifting of the robot's metallic legs echoed on the white tile floor as it came out from a passage inside the wall. The doctor had done her job and left to tend to another patient.

The robot approached between the stirrups and focused its hollow gaze upon the unconscious teen. On its forehead was the number "F66." From one of its elongated hands, it produced a finger that was a sharp scalpel. The other fingers were soft prongs. Its chest opened and produced a medium-size glass cylinder that it retrieved with its other hand. The cylinder had metal ends and a small clear bulb embedded in it. Wires appeared to float inside the liquid. The robot opened one side of the cylinder and then scanned the teen once more. It was ready to retrieve its target.

The procedure took only a few minutes. The robot delicately retrieved the fetus and the placenta as one. It placed it in the cylinder and closed the lid. The fetus was preserved whole, intact and alive. Its life source now came from the cylinder and the nutrients in the liquid.

The robot's chest opened once again to receive its prize. Once the fetus was inside the robot, the robot tended to the teen for a few more minutes. Then it placed its hands in an opening in its sides to sanitize itself.

When F66 was done, it turned and walked toward the wall. The passage opened automatically to let it through, then closed again. The teen was left in the room, alone and unconscious.

* —— ✦ —— *

The wall opened into a long hallway. The walls, the floor, and the ceiling were made of stainless steel. Other robots plodded along to the sound of air being released from their hydraulic limbs. Some were headed toward patients' doorways while others walked in the same direction as F66.

F66 reached the end of the hallway, then slowed as it approached several other robots unloading their cylinders onto a rack that was on a conveyor belt. F66 waited its turn. When it was time, its chest opened, and it reached inside to retrieve the cylinder.

The rack held twelve cylinders, and F66 placed its cylinder into the rack to make a dozen. F66 stepped back as a covering descended over the cylinders, followed by the injection of a blue liquid.

The bulb on F66's cylinder began to blink immediately, signaling life and adaptation. This had never occurred so quickly. F66 noted it and paused as it digitally logged the information for a future report regarding the abnormalities.

The covering retreated, and the rack rolled away, replaced by another one. F66 turned and went to retrieve another empty container. As it did, another robot stepped into its place to place its cylinder into the new rack.

F66 placed the new container into the compartment in its chest and plodded back down the hallway to retrieve another subject.

Meanwhile, another cylinder on the rolling rack began to blink faintly. It would soon grow stronger, and it would only be a short time before a few more joined in. In fact, on average only four of the twelve would take to the blue liquid and survive, a fate to be determined within a matter of minutes. The rest would be considered expired and be discarded, used for research or their tissue recycled for other uses.

The rack continued until it came to rest in front of a machine that removed the cylinders. Five of the twelve lights were blinking. The machine separated the vials with blinking lights and placed them in a separate blue rack until the rack was filled. Then it was placed on a different conveyor belt. The others were sent down a chute, the containers to be recycled.

Eventually, the rack rolled into a small open hangar. Large security robots were stationed inside. A lone vehicle was parked with the back hatch open to receive its cargo. One the side of the vehicle was written "The Gamble Corporation-In Service to the Western Alliance and European Union (WAEU)" in bold artistic lettering. Beneath it was written "The New World Order-We're building a better world for tomorrow." Next to this lettering were the symbols of the Gamble Corporation and the WAEU.

A thin man was standing next to a larger man. They conversed while the racks were automatically transported into the vehicle from the machines. Both were wearing beige jumpsuits with matching caps.

"They say more than half of these won't make it to nine months," the larger man said. "But those that do—"

"Be quiet," the thin man said in a hushed voice. "You know we can be killed for talking about it."

"Only to outsiders."

"Even so, we need to be careful discussing it. I don't want to be misunderstood, even if it's just us."

"The original ones should be about ten years old by now. Have you ever seen one of them?"

"No, but I heard they have freakish eyes because of the TS gene injections, whatever that is. Too bad it kills most of them before they even get started."

"It's not only the eyes but their hair. I had to deliver something to Mr. Gascon a couple of years ago and caught a glimpse of one during an isolated drill. He was just a little guy, but I swear he already had the skills of a well-trained soldier. His speed and execution were inhuman."

"Freaks," the thinner man said.

"*Our* freaks," the larger man replied. "But they need to be to take on the Mandarin Kingdom."

The thinner man paused in thought for a few moments. Then he returned his gaze to the larger man. "Think we'll go to war?"

His partner nodded. "It's inevitable."

The two continued to converse until the signal was given that there were no more to be loaded.

"It's time to go," the larger man said, giving the command to close the hatch.

His partner complied, and the two entered the vehicle. Seatbelts automatically secured them. "The cargo is confirmed and accounted for," the vehicle's intercom voice said. "Proceed to Los Angeles sector nine, Gamble Portal twenty-six."

"Bearings set, exit building," the driver said.

The vehicle rose with a slight turn, and the hangar door opened. Then the vehicle took off to connect to the grid.

"I still don't understand," said the thinner man. "I mean, aren't they still human? How will they be able to defeat Mandarin robots if they're human like us?"

"There's a lot you don't know. No matter how we advance in technology, the human element will always be greater. When they're ready, no machine will be able to stand in their way."

The thinner man smirked. "Kind of strange, isn't it?"

"What's that?"

"These citizens didn't find them valuable, yet they're valuable to us all."

"Yes, I guess if you put it that way. The ones who survive anyway. We're doing a great work. Those of them who stay alive from this batch may become our lifeline."

The thinner man nodded knowingly.

"Change is coming," the larger man continued. "Soon the world will come to know them well. The ways of warfare will have to adapt. The Featral are here to stay."

THE CHALLENGE

THE YEAR WAS 2109.

LIGHT STREAKED THROUGH the forest, reflecting off those seated on the ground below the trees. Several figures dressed in metallic black sat in a row, five males and two females. The humidity was high, but it seemed to have no effect on them. There was no evidence of perspiration or discomfort.

Their fitted armored-plated uniforms validated the essence of supremacy and order. They were in training, part of the WAEU ground forces, Featral special ops Golden Eagle. They were armed with different types of explosives and magnetic grenade devices fastened to their uniforms. Each wore a light transparent headset and clear interactive glasses. On their command, the glasses automatically connected from the sides of their heads and over the middle of their noses. Their legs were crossed, as were their arms. In each hand, proton laser guns were unlocked and ready.

Surgically implanted as a flat small silver circle on the lower part of their heads, near their right ears, was the cybernetically attached Bohmian device

. The device had been implanted in them at around age five. Initially, it made them sick for weeks, until their brains and the cells in their bodies adjusted. The intrusiveness would have killed a normal person immediately. However, the Featral had what others didn't, the adaptation to the TS gene.

The gene gave their skin a slightly bluish tone, as was the case with their fingernails. Their skin adapted to the extreme changes in temperature and resisted harmful radiation. The color of their hair varied from mid to darker shades of blue. But what stood out most was the royal-blue color that replaced the whites of their eyes. In fact, their eyeballs were completely blue. Their irises and pupils not visible.

To those observing them, the Featral's speed, and reflexes were superhuman. But from the Featral's point of view, it was time itself that slowed. Basic muscle strength was also increased.

This group of Featral had been through similar drills before. However, this time was different. This was the final phase before they would be officially released to join others in warfare and special operations.

Their proton lasers were set on level three on a five-level spectrum. This was also true for the weaponry of their simulated opposition. The setting was enough to cause a slight burn and some swelling in the target. The opposing robots were set to respond to contact at this level. Explosions were another matter and had to be directed and monitored to avoid massive injury.

Behind the seven seated Featral was a two-story building with a large extended glass window on the second level. An invisible force field protected the building from the activities that were about to take place. Two men in white lab coats stood behind the glass, along with a military captain.

The captain, who was dressed in camouflage, had been sent there to monitor their progress. He had a specific interest with this team, particularly their leader. Miniature holographic images were displayed around the conference table. The images displayed the participants below and their surrounding environment. As was standard, the images were being broadcast to training facilities where other Featral were watching.

Mr. Humphrey sat carefully monitoring the holographic program.

The captain looked up from his information Cronepad. "How long until the robots attack?"

"Two minutes and thirty-eight seconds, Captain Johnson," Humphrey replied. He turned and continued to focus on the task before him.

Captain Johnson stepped next to the other man. "So, Dr. Snider, which is the one you were telling me about?"

"Socrates," Snider replied. "Our bluish-white male third from the left. He's their crew leader. The African American next to him is the L2. Watch out for him as well." Dr. Snider looked back out of the window. "Socrates," he said, snickering. "I always wondered about their names and how they came by them."

"I assure you, the names given are more random than you think," Johnson replied.

"Random or not," Humphrey said, "Socrates is better than anything we've ever seen so far. He's been perfect for the past four years now."

"What do you mean perfect?"

"He's one hundred percent with no injuries to his person," Humphrey replied. "Basically, the bots and drones don't get to him. They also rarely get to his team once his team senses his location spots and movements. They efficiently evolve around him in battle. It's funny; others in camp already defer to him out of respect."

"That may not be a good thing," Johnson replied. "I know they've been trained as a team, but if he goes down the others on his team may be at a disadvantage. Could they function under another leader? One individual should not gain that much supremacy over the others."

"They might under the L2," Humphrey said.

Dr. Snider turned to Johnson and narrowed his gaze. "Well, we got something for him today."

Humphrey nodded approvingly and noted the time. "They'll be in range in thirty seconds."

The seated Featral all had their heads down, listening and maintaining their focus. To Socrates' left was a muscular but sleek female fighter of Asian descent who went by the name of Kanga. To his right was an African American male named Ton. Ton was the L2, the second in command.

Socrates heard them first. He tilted his head and spoke into his headset. Digital information appeared on his glasses. "Nano air-drones 35NW.022, Mandarin ground bots SE, 45SW." As he spoke into his headset, others began speaking simultaneously over each other. However, they all received and understood the information each other gave. After several seconds, they had their bearings.

Time slowed…

Assessment and calculated action occurred within a second. As one, they moved instantaneously from their seated positions. Without bracing himself, Socrates rose to a standing position. While doing so, he twisted his body around and uncrossed his arms and legs. Shots fired from both of his lasers at the approaching bots.

Simultaneously, Kanga rolled forward to her feet and sprinted away, firing as she ran.

Others parted, firing in the same fashion.

The robots were upon them, simulated Mandarin robots. Each was shaped like and had the basic movements of an eight-foot-tall man. Lasers were attached to their robotic hands and were mounted on their right shoulders.

The Featral were fast. However, the robots were also swift, and they didn't go down easily. Sometimes it took several shots to disable them. However, a few direct hits to the head and torso worked well on a Mandarin bot.

The Featral used the cover of the trees to their advantage. Shots flooded the area, streams of light flashing past them as they returned fire.

Kanga was on the run. Avoiding a laser blast, she leaped into the air, firing a shot before flipping in a tucked position and springing back to her feet. As she did, she connected two shots to a bot's head, causing it to buckle backward. Debris flew as the bot became disabled. Then she rolled for cover behind a tree.

Ton attacked another beside the disabled bot before he digitally noted the incoming swarm of insect nanobots.

Socrates was already sprinting past him. He holstered one of his guns and reached to his shoulder for a palm-sized magnetic grenade. As he ran past Ton, he set the charge and flung it into the air. The magnetic grenade exploded into a light mist that the nanobots instantly gravitated toward. Sparks flashed within the mist due to contact with the tiny bots. Socrates ducked behind another large tree not far from Kanga and retrieved his weapon.

Shots whizzed past him, sending chunks of bark flying. A barrage of laser fire from the Mandarin robots lit up the tree where Socrates was. He looked at the singed mark on the tree and raised an eyebrow. Then he noted that none of the shots fired had been directed at Kanga. Something had changed. The others were only being subjected to return fire from robot defensive tactics. The attack appeared to be directed at Socrates. He raised his head to detect and reassess the enemy.

"The bots have a lock on you, L1," Ton said over the comms. "Get out of there! They're trying to take you out of the equation!"

"They must have changed the simulation from above," Kanga replied.

"I'll be the bait," Socrates said. "Focus on one bot coming after me at a time. Don't go after my targets. I'll take care of them."

Kanga gave him a glare but then nodded.

To cover him, Featral shot at incoming bots who were pounding the tree where Socrates was.

Time slowed again...

In a blur, Socrates took off in an easterly direction. It took a few moments for the bots to realize their target had moved. Kanga and the others immediately went after one of the bots trailing him.

Socrates ran toward an isolated bot, changing direction frequently at an amazing speed. The bots' shots continued to miss.

Simultaneously, he fired shots that connected to a bot several times. As he got closer, the last two shots to the head of the Mandarin bot finally caused it to stagger. It attempted to gather itself until another shot caused it to fall to its knees.

It continued to shoot, but Socrates somersaulted high over the bot's head with a half twist, avoiding another stream of blasts that came from a distance. While upside down directly over it, he fired directly into the bot's skull, disabling it. He landed directly behind it and used the bot for cover, absorbing another flurry of blasts. Then he ran off into the hilly terrain.

Meanwhile, the others had already disabled three of the bots who had attempted to chase Socrates.

Dr. Snider was incensed as he watched from above. "There's no way he can do that. He's cheating somehow. I know it."

"He's always beaten our simulations in the past," Humphrey replied. "Why is today any different?"

"I'm very impressed with Socrates and this team," Johnson said. "But recently Mandarin forces have implemented their bots on flyers. Are you able to simulate that?"

"We only have three functional flyers at the moment," Humphrey replied. "The Featral should have an easy time with the exposed aerial targets though. But if that's what you want, we'll call the bots off, regroup, and activate the flyers. It will only take a few minutes."

Johnson nodded in agreement.

Humphrey ordered the remainder of the robots to retreat and reassemble. The loudspeaker informed the Featral to stand down and return.

Dr. Snider narrowed his eyes and looked down with disdain as Socrates' team regrouped and stood in a line with their weapons holstered. Socrates called for the roll call. When they were done, they all sat down, legs crossed as before.

Minutes passed. Dr. Snider continued to look down with an angry stare. "Socrates," he mumbled.

"Are you alright, Doctor?" Humphrey asked.

"How long?"

"Five minutes and thirty-nine seconds, Doctor."

The flyers were the same standard flyers that were used by Mandarin Forces as well as the WAEU. They were modeled after the two-seat jet ski watercraft of the 2030s. These airborne craft were light, and coupled with the strong compulsion from its engines, were easily maneuverable, particularly in short spaces.

Dr. Snider approached Humphrey, lowering his voice. "They have studied the makeup of the flyers and know exactly where to direct their fire, correct?"

Humphrey nodded. "The flyers will be easy targets for them." He looked up. "Set the bots and the flyers at level five."

Humphrey turned to the doctor in alarm. "You know that's not allowed. The second I alert the Featral to set at level five, Captain Johnson will have a fit."

"I didn't say anything about telling the Featral to change their settings or alerting Captain Johnson."

"But-"

"Just do it," Dr. Snider snapped through clenched teeth.

The exchange caused Johnson to look up from his Cronepad. "Is everything alright?"

After a moment's pause, Humphrey turned back to the task before him. "Yes, Captain. We're regrouping. The flyers will be ready shortly."

"Very good."

The Featral sensed the incoming ground bots and began communicating as before, readying their weapons. As the bots approached for another attack, Socrates noted the flyers but waited to see how long it would take one of his team members to report them. About three seconds later, Kanga reported three flyers were approaching.

Keeping their spacing, Kanga led three of the Featral to the right, sprinting to their positions.

Socrates and two others moved toward the incoming bots.

Ton trailed behind to adjust based upon the opposition's reaction.

The flyers hummed in linear unison before making their descent. Each one was equipped with a laser cannon and was manned by a Mandarin bot. Ground bots rushed in and attacked as before.

A violent exchange of laser fire commenced. Singed chunks of dirt flew up as the blasts from the laser cannons pummeled the ground.

The Featral knew there were certain ventilation spots where the flyers could be damaged, breaking the bots' control over them. They knew exactly where to shoot. Despite the speed and fierceness of the aerial attack, taking out the flyers was much easier than taking out the Mandarin ground bots. The flyers' speed was not an issue.

However, Socrates was alerted that something was different due to the level of explosiveness coming from the flyers' cannons. At first, he thought it might be part of the realistic simulation, but he became increasingly suspicious after his team connected several times with a passing flyer. One of them fired several shots into a ventilation opening, with little effect. Socrates also scored some direct hits on the flyer. After a brief sputter, it looped around for another approach.

Meanwhile, Kanga and the others were having trouble with ground bots and another low-flying flyer.

L6, the other female Featral on the team, assumed from experience that her shots would disable the bot, then turned her attention to another. It was an unfortunate mistake. The bot was not disabled, and she was hit.

Kanga turned to see a series of light bursts pound her downed Featral partner. With each blast, L6's body jolted. "L6 is down!" she shouted. "Featral terminated!"

"Terminated?" Ton replied.

With a narrow focus, Kanga kept moving.

"Level five!" Socrates shouted over the headset.

They all complied.

Socrates now understood they had not been fighting with forces of equal weaponry. Because they had not been warned, it had cost them one of their own.

Dr. Snider snickered behind his thick glasses.

"What just happened?" Captain Johnson exclaimed.

"Looks like one of them got careless," Snider replied.

"Call it off. I don't want any more going down."

"It's too late for that one. But it looks like they have already figured it out anyway," Humphrey observed.

"It's the perfect simulation, Captain. The threat is real." Dr. Snider's eye twitched. "Errors in execution will end in death."

Johnson didn't like it, but he withdrew his protest as he gazed at the scene outside. A heightened level of ferocity permeated the backdrop of the laser blast. Kanga avoided oncoming fire and let off a flurry of shots at a passing flyer's ventilation opening. The flyer sputtered out of control and exploded into a nearby tree.

With their weapons at level five, they were able to dispense with the enemy as before. There was much more violence and wreckage. However, the outcome of the battle was going the same way as before.

Socrates knew his team was upset, but he urged them to stay focused.

Meanwhile, other Featral in training watched over the broadcasts and tried to interpret the activities. They had seen death in simulations before. However, the only time level five was used was for disciplinary reasons. That Featral would be allowed a challenge to redeem themselves. However, none ever survived.

Before the Featral finished off the rest of the bots, Humphrey called the bots back and ordered the Featral to stand down.

"Roll call," Socrates ordered.

The seven were now six. The body was dragged away by workers wearing protective gear to shield them from the heat and humidity.

The stress on Socrates' team had increased. None of them moved to wipe the perspiration that had formed on their foreheads. The strain could be seen on their hardened faces as they responded to the roll call, their eyes facing forward.

"Well, I've seen enough," Johnson said. "This group is more than ready. I'm going to commission them as soon as possible. It's a shame we lost one. Stand them down. I'm going down to examine the body for my report. Then I'll contact headquarters."

Dr. Snider continued to mumble under his breath.

Humphrey acknowledged the captain as he left the room to put on his protective clothing.

Dr. Snider secured the door behind him. An invisible security force field, which was only known to the two of them, was activated, securing the room. Dr. Snider turned to Humphrey. "Dismiss everyone but Socrates."

"Doctor?"

"Why am I repeating myself to you? Socrates has embarrassed me for the last time."

Humphrey turned and gave the order over his headset.

"After that escapade of destruction, what do we have left?"

"There are about thirteen bots left. The destruction from this simulation will set us back about six weeks at least."

"Send them all at him, level five."

"Doctor, you heard the captain. I don't think that's wise. The outside simulations are broadcast automatically to the training facilities. What will they think? Besides, Socrates has done nothing wrong."

"Do you want to keep your job, Humphrey? His error is setting himself above the others. Such power needs to be controlled, or it will be used against us. Don't you understand? This will be a reminder that we are in control. That's what they will think. Now do it!"

When the order to dispense with Socrates was given, the Featral glanced at each other, their eyes hesitant.

"What are they trying to do?" Ton asked under his breath.

"What does it mean, L1?" Kanga said.

Socrates made no movement. He simply issued an order. "Comply."

"But we did what they asked us to do," Kanga said.

"Comply," Socrates responded more sharply.

Ton sneered. Then they all arose and left to the building where their team member's body had been dragged. As they walked away, each, in turn, looked back toward their team leader, who remained focused and seated.

The team gathered where her body had been laid.

Captain Johnson had come down to meet them. He briefly examined the body. "We didn't intend to have fatalities as part of these drills. We'll have to reassess these modules." He looked at Ton. "You have all fought admirably and will be commissioned." Johnson noted that Socrates was not with them. He looked back and saw that he was in the ready position seated where they had left him. "Why is your team leader not with you?"

The Featral looked at one another before Ton responded. "You don't know? We were dispensed with except for him."

"It's a challenge," Kanga scoffed, turning her head. The others ignored the fact that her comment was out of order, Ton's rank allowing him to address Captain Johnson.

"I didn't order that," Johnson replied. While he was still speaking, Socrates opened fire, running toward approaching bots who had fired upon him. How Socrates survived the first few moments of the exchange, the captain didn't know. He immediately got on his link to Dr. Snider and Humphrey. "What are you doing? Call them off now!"

Humphrey received the call from Johnson. He looked up at Dr. Snider, who simply ordered the communication link between them closed.

"Call them off now!" Johnson repeated. "That's an order!" There was no response. The Featral pulled their weapons and readied to charge. However, before they moved, Ton held up his hand to stop them. "The force field has been put back up! We can't get through." He waved to Kanga. "L3, the control room!" Kanga immediately took two others with her to break in up the stairwell.

The others looked on helplessly, unable to assist Socrates. A minute later, Kanga's voice came over the comms to Ton. "There's a second field in front of the door that extends out to the walls."

Ton scanned the area.

Johnson knew the Featral were already ahead of him, but he said it anyway. "We must knock out the power source to penetrate the force field."

"Searching," Kanga replied. She looked up at the ceiling. "Let's open up this ceiling a bit." She nodded to the other two. They stepped back and used their lasers to blast a large opening in the ceiling.

Socrates was still engaged in his personal war with Mandarin bots. He had to focus more than ever before. His life depended on it. Socrates was pushed beyond the limits of concentration. Because of his swiftness, the bots continued to fire where he was not. At the same time, the impact of level-five laser shots was more devastating.

One of the laser streams hit a bot, causing its circuits to ignite and explode. In Socrates' mind, time not only slowed, it almost came to a complete stop. Parts floated in midair. Socrates holstered one of his weapons in the blink of an eye. A part flew off from within the bot's arm. It was a thick three-foot metal bar that curved on the end like a hook. In one swift motion, Socrates snatched the bar and swung it, hitting the bot's head and shoulders. He flipped the bot around and ripped out wires and parts. Before the bot collapsed to the ground, it fired off a flurry of blasts, hitting another nearby bot and disabling it.

◆———◆———◆

Those who were watching were astonished by Socrates' violent disposal of the Mandarin bots against what looked like impossible odds. There was also confusion as to why this was occurring. The broadcast was too captivating to ignore, and it was too late to cut off without laying a further seed of discord. This Featral was doing things they had never seen before. He was meeting their challenge and succeeding.

◆———◆———◆

After a few minutes, Socrates disposed of the final four bots in quick order. He was now a distance from the main building. He looked around and noted no further activity. Then he sat, his arms and legs crossed in the ready position once again. Sweat mixed with blood from the scrapes and cuts on his cheek as he waited for whatever was next.

◆———◆———◆

Debris from the ceiling littered the floor, and dust and smoke filled the air. A large opening exposed what was above it. Kanga leaped to the opening and made her way through. Another Featral followed her as the remaining one stayed behind.

Above the ceiling, there was enough room to stand upright. Even though the light was dim, the Featral were able to see through it. The force field extended up past the ceiling. Several metal boxes were affixed to different spots on the wall, each displaying blinking lights. Cables and pipes were also strung along from one place to another. After a quick assessment, they fired at the boxes and cables.

———◆———

"Socrates!" Dr. Snider exclaimed, clenching his fist. "We have a missile, a short-range mini for the defense of the grounds. Kill him!"

"Doctor, you've lost it!

"I don't care! You don't get it. Killing that Featral is for our defense. Kill him!"

"We're already in trouble. I won't do it. Besides, we only have one, and it took months to get it in here. I'm shutting this down." Humphrey turned and began to deactivate his board.

They both paused when they heard what appeared to be shots and crumbling plaster coming from the wall and ceiling next to them. The lights flickered.

Dr. Snider rushed to a nearby drawer and retrieved a hand laser. It took a few seconds to warm up to level five.

Humphrey figured he was arming himself against the pending invasion and turned back to complete his task of deactivation. Suddenly, Humphrey's head jolted forward and thudded onto the desk. Dr. Snider had shot Humphrey in the back of his head. A trail of vapor rose from the scorched fatal wound.

Dr. Snider knew his time was running short. Their secure setup had been compromised. He looked out the window toward Socrates and then prepared the missile for launch.

As Ton looked out, there was a moment of relief. Socrates appeared to be uninjured. Then the depowering sound from the outside field could be heard by all. L4 looked at Ton and nodded.

"L1, the force field to the outer building is down," Ton reported.

"The one inside the door is still activated but doesn't cover the outer glass," Kanga said over the comms.

Socrates stood up and turned his head toward the building and tilted his head toward the sky. Suddenly, Socrates sprinted toward the building.

The ground lifted behind him with a violently combustible swell of earth and fire. Although he was far ahead where the projectile hit, the impact propelled his body forward, and he crashed and rolled several times.

Meanwhile, Captain Johnson hurriedly joined the Featral. With the outer force field down, they gathered out in front of the building to focus laser shots on the building's thick glass. It heated up to an orange glow, cracked, and then shattered.

Ton and another Featral began to climb up.

Kanga swung down from the top.

Snider knew he was doomed. It only took seconds.

Kanga blasted the board. Then Ton shot Snider, killing him.

Below, Socrates stood up and brushed himself off. Besides some scrapes and bruises, he was uninjured. He walked over and stood near Johnson. They both looked up as Ton dragged Dr. Snider's body to the edge and threw it out. Another Featral did the same with Humphrey's body. Both bodies landed in front of Johnson and Socrates.

"Sir, the threat has been terminated!" Ton yelled, retracted his glasses as he looked down from the broken window.

Everyone knew Ton was speaking to Socrates, not Johnson. Socrates gave Ton a stern nod in return. Then he turned and glared at the captain.

For those Featral who were watching, the injustice of humanity had just been broadcast, but one of their own had beaten back the challenge. From that day forward, Socrates would be esteemed as "Socrates Challenge."

He retracted his glasses from his face and walked away from the captain. He spoke into his headset.

"Roll call."

THE CALL OF DUTY

HOUSTON - WAEU MILITARY BASE
ARMY AND AERIAL COMMAND

LEANNA WAS A Featral of Latin descent. She was fit, as were all the Featral around her. However, she didn't have an athletic build like the ground troops. Her build, intellect, and reflexes made her a prime candidate to excel in the Featral Air Force. She was number one in her sector and ranked third amongst all the trainees in her class. Leanna was also known to have a feisty edge, which was part of what made her successful as a pilot. At times though it worked against her.

Leanna stood in line in the cafeteria, her arms folded and her fingers tapping impatiently on her bicep. When it was her turn, she stepped onto the platform that read her weight. Then the computer analyzed the food and supplements to be distributed.

She was grateful that the TS gene made it so that a Featral virtually never became sick. All food distribution was calculated for maximum efficiency, health, and strength. She had been told that it was necessary for her to have consistent weight to be a pilot. She was weighed once a week, normally in relation to one of her meals.

"You have gained two pounds," the computer blurted.

So what? Leanna thought, though she dared not say it. *That's why I'm still flying a plane instead of a stupid machine like you doing it. I can fly circles around any drone, two extra pounds or not!*

The computer delayed processing, seemingly reading her displeasure. Finally, it dispensed the meal—a few discolored vegetables and a personalized dinner bar. She rolled her eyes at the unappetizing meal and then retrieved her water and went to sit at the table with a male Featral pilot. He acknowledged Leanna as she sat. She noted his meal was as dull as her own.

"I heard one of them say something about a steak being pretty tasty. Ever had a steak, Leanna?"

"Of course not," she snapped.

"Well, I guess since they don't have to be us, they don't have to eat like us either."

"Well, we have to be perfect to kill on their behalf, don't we?" Leanna said with a sarcasm that bordered insubordination. She took a bite of the dinner bar. Then she held it out and looked at it. "Maybe it would taste better if they changed the color or something."

He smirked. "Only in your imagination. You're just a number here. Your value is flying. That's it."

Leanna scoffed.

He continued to eat his own dinner bar. Then he looked around and leaned in close. "Hey, have you heard the skinny?" he whispered.

"What?"

"The Challenge and his team will be shipping out from this facility. In fact, they're probably already here."

"How do you know?"

"There's a grounder called Max. He's the Featral over the Orange Barracks on the north side. I was waiting inside their commander's office to deliver a message. Max was waiting there too. Apparently, he had been there earlier and had returned a second time. We were the only two in the room. He was very upset. He said the Challenge should get more respect. When I asked him what he meant, he said the Challenge and his team were going to be housed in the Orange Barracks until they received their assignment. I guess he saw in my face my concern that he had just breached confidentiality. Max told me not to worry. He said they didn't deem it important enough to keep it confidential."

"Are we able to see him?"

"I suppose there's nothing stopping you from going over there if you have a break in your duties. I certainly don't."

"Well, I have a little down time tonight before curfew."

The pilot shook his head and then rushed to finish the last part of his crusty dinner bar. Then he grabbed his tray and stood up. "I have to get going. I hope you get a chance to meet him before you're deployed. Maybe we'll both get lucky and be sent to where his team is going."

She smiled and nodded. As he left to dispose of his tray, Leanna chewed her dinner bar and mulled over the events she had seen on the broadcast. Every time she thought about it, a sense of pride filled her. This was not the same pride as an accomplishment well done or her excelling over other pilots during drills. It was a sense of pride in who she was, in her identity. Socrates Challenge made her proud to be a Featral. She knew others felt the same.

It was about a five-minute ride to the Orange Barracks on the north side. However, she didn't have access to a vehicle. If she couldn't figure out a way to get there, she would have to go on foot.

Leanna didn't know how long she would have to live after being deployed in battle. The end of her life was simply not a concern, but she sensed that whatever life she did have would be more meaningful having met the one who had given her a reason to be proud.

She had to meet Socrates Challenge.

◆———◆———◆

After cleaning up and getting medical attention, Socrates' team boarded a plane that transported them to the Houston base. They arrived at about 3:00 p.m. There was a lull of fifteen minutes during which the team sat inside the hangar on benches, waiting for their ground transportation. Military civilians and officers bustled back and forth. Because Featral were trained at the base, nobody paid them any special attention. They were tired, and they waited in silence.

Across the way, Socrates caught sight of a woman with a baby stroller. She was young and wearing jeans and a white blouse. She was also wearing makeup, as non-Featral women sometimes did, including lipstick. She was waiting as well but with an urgent of expectancy. The toddler waved a rattle back and forth, occasionally making sounds that were not quite words. When the woman saw that she was being observed, she pulled the stroller closer to her.

Socrates picked up on the subtle inclination of the mother's protectiveness. *How ironic that the same protectiveness was not afforded to the Featral.* He glanced at his team. *All of us were discarded to be terminated by them.* He turned back to look at her with indifference.

After a while, some officers arrived. One broke off from the group and went over to where the woman was. She pushed the stroller toward him, and they embraced. He lifted her off the ground and kissed her. Then he took the toddler out of the stroller. He held the baby up and twirled him around, to the toddler's delight.

The woman looked back over at the Featral and then whispered something in the man's ear. He looked at them and then put the baby in the stroller. They hugged again and then walked away together.

Just then a male officer in uniform pulled up to the Featral on an opened passenger vehicle. He waved to Socrates and his team. "I was ordered to pick you up and take you to the Orange Barracks. Hop in!"

The Featral boarded, and they drove off.

Once they reached the barracks, they were given a subsection inside that was separated by a shoulder-high partition. Apparently, some Featral had been alerted to their presence and who they were. This caused a commotion. However, despite the bustle around them, his team would have no problem sleeping.

As Socrates laid down, he thought about the death of his team member. He glanced around at the others and wondered how many days each had left. Some might not survive the battle to come, or maybe the one after that. All of them would eventually see death, himself included. They could not delay the inevitable. Nonetheless, Socrates was pleased by the way his team had met the day's challenge. They would need this experience in the future, however long that would be.

He was cognizant of some Featral looking over the partition to stare. Socrates didn't mind and didn't say a word. He simply turned and closed his eyes, resting along with his team.

◆——◆——◆

Leanna had finished her drills for the evening and was standing outside of her barrack overlooking a dimly lit dirt road. She had a small pack on her back, and she was wearing a tight black beanie with fitted black gloves. The road she was on would lead her to the north side.

The temperature dropped drastically from a hot and unbearable day to a chilling evening. The slight frost from the evening breeze blew across her face. The warmth from her breath blew vapors into the night air. She looked down at her shoes which contrasted with the ground, then looked back up, her piercing blue eyes focused on the road ahead. Then Leanna began to run.

Dirt kicked up behind her with her first few steps. Leanna quickly built up her pace to a sprint. Her blue hair flew in the wind from beneath her beanie.

The ability to maintain a sprint for a long period of time was impossible for a normal person, but to a trained Featral, it was standard. She was not in the same type of shape as the grounders. However, this distance would be no problem for her.

She whizzed past those who were walking, both Featral and non-Featral alike. Neither were concerned at the sight of her running by them. As she maintained her pace, she felt the cool air rush across her face. She turned her head ever so slightly to the bend of the road that curved around the corner.

With each gliding stride, anticipation built inside her. She hadn't had such feelings since the day she first flew a plane. She had always thought of herself simply as an agent to fight off evil on behalf of her overseers. However, thoughts of being special now rolled through her mind.

As the Orange Barracks came into view, she slowed to a halt. When she did, she noticed a couple of Featral standing at the entrance, conversing. One was a tall male African American Featral and the other was a shorter male Featral of Asian descent. Leanna was not winded, but the pace of her breathing was faster than normal. The two Featral at the entrance had detected her approach from afar, observing her with a curious understanding.

"There's another one, Ben," the African American Featral said.

"Yup. Another one, Ron," said the Asian Featral.

"Another one of what?" Leanna responded sarcastically between breaths.

"You're obviously not a grounder," said Ben.

"Why do you say that?"

"You couldn't have come from that far, and you have to catch your breath."

"And you are wearing a knit hat. It's thirty-eight degrees. It's not cold enough to resort to a knit hat," said Ron.

Feeling self-conscious, she pulled off her hat and tried to regain control over her breathing. "I'm a fighter pilot."

"A fighter pilot," Ron replied unenthusiastically.

Leanna ignored the slight and stepped closer. "Is the Challenge and his team here?"

"They are," Ben replied.

She looked past them and noticed it was crowded inside. "May I go in?"

"I'm sure you can squeeze your way through," Ben said. "They haven't awakened yet, but you can go in."

She nodded confidently and then stepped past them. "Thank you."

Inside, Featral were crammed close to one another. Some were in their distinctive informal dress, which distinguished them as ground troops. Everyone's Bohmian devices reflected throughout the dim room. This was also true for Leanna.

Most remained quiet. Those who did talk did so in whispers, trying not to disturb their sleeping comrades.

Leanna maneuvered through the crowd to where she could see the team over the partition. She noted a few of them were awake but still lying down. The female seemed to be staring blankly in her direction. It felt like her blue gaze was fixed on Leanna. Leanna knew that wasn't the case. However, she believed everyone standing in the same area probably had the same impression. The female was so still that Leanna could not tell if she was breathing, nor could she detect even a blink. She also noted this female was the only one visibly armed.

She figured them lying there had something to do with some sort of team protocol. From what Leanna deduced from the broadcast, the one with his back turned to her had to be Socrates Challenge.

Ten minutes passed, and the female still did not move. However, Socrates finally did. He sat up, glanced at the gathering, and then addressed his team.

✦ —✦— ✦

"Are you awake, L2?" Socrates asked.

Ton opened his eyes and stretched his limbs. "I am now, L1." Ton did a quick scan of his immediate area to note the other team members, who were sitting up in response to Socrates' voice. "All are here and accounted for, L1."

"Our crowd seems to have grown," Socrates said.

Just then, one of the bystanders approached, others trailing behind him. Socrates recognized a noted deference to this Featral, who the others viewed as a commander. Socrates and his team, and those around, started to stand at attention but he waved them off.

"I am Quentarius, Featral Commander Twelve, Central Command."

Socrates knew this was the highest command a Featral could obtain. Tens of thousands were technically under his command, although he wouldn't have much say when final decisions were made. Socrates wondered why he was there addressing them. Socrates and his team acknowledged his presence.

Before Quentarius continued, he winced to cover some sort of physical discomfort. The gesture was ever so slight, but Socrates picked up on it.

"We're very proud of your accomplishments," Quentarius said. "Tomorrow at 0900, you and your second in command have been ordered to join me to be briefed on a mission. This mission will require Featral special ops. Your team was selected. That is all I can say right now. You will be picked up at 0830. Formal dress is expected."

"Understood," Socrates replied.

"Good. With the formalities out of the way, I know there are many here who want to meet you and your team. If you need anything now or in the future, please let me know. We're very resourceful."

"Thank you, sir."

"No, thank you, Socrates Challenge."

After Quentarius stepped back, other Featral came forward to introduce themselves. Everyone was polite and cordial, engaging in brief conversation. They all were cognizant that time was limited and that many others were there. Socrates' crew didn't appear to think much of all the attention, particularly Kanga. However, Socrates was being diplomatic, and they followed his lead.

While Socrates was exchanging greetings, he noticed a small commotion. Two Featral were arguing with each other. One was a female. The female seemed upset and was pointing at the other with a balled-up knit hat in her hand.

"Is everything alright over there?" Socrates asked.

"Yes, everything is fine," Leanna replied, somewhat embarrassed for having drawn attention to herself.

The other nodded and then whispered to her. "Well, go ahead then."

Socrates smiled to himself as Leanna stepped forward behind the group who had been conversing with him and the rest of his team. However, everything stopped as Leanna approached.

"I'm sorry about the disruption," Leanna said. "I came here on foot. My barrack is at the other end of the facility. I have to get back before curfew."

Socrates looked out beyond her. "Is Quentarius still here?"

"Yes," Ben responded. "He's outside."

"Can you ask him if he has someone available to rush this Featral back to her quarters?"

Ben nodded and then went outside to catch Quentarius.

"And you are?" Socrates asked.

"Oh, I'm sorry, I'm Leanna. I'm a fighter pilot."

Socrates shook her hand. "Pleased to meet you, Leanna."

"It's my honor, sir. I really admire what you did against their unjust challenge. And I'm sorry for the loss of one of your team." She nodded toward Ton and the others.

"Thank you," Socrates replied.

Just then Ben came in and waved at them.

"I believe your ride is ready," Socrates said.

"Thank you. Thank you very much. It was a pleasure meeting you, sir." She backed away and made her way through the crowd toward the entrance. Before exiting, she paused to look back at Socrates one more time.

Socrates made eye contact with her and smiled. Something about her appealed to him. He got the impression this wouldn't be the last time he saw her.

Then Leanna turned to leave the barracks and catch her ride.

◆——◆——◆

-MEANWHILE IN LOS ANGELES-
SECTOR 7-GAMBLE CORPORATION FACILITY

Sirens screamed within the facility's walls. The cameras had lost their function, and the power was out. Backup generators were down and would not kick in.

Several guards rushed downstairs into the dark hallway, their lasers drawn. Their scopes reflected beams of light off the walls and floor.

One of the beams reflected off the mangled body of a guard. A small pool of blood reflected beneath his torso. They proceeded farther down the hall. Several more bodies were exposed in the same manner, guards, and scientists alike. The commander noted that their fatal wounds seemed to have been inflicted by the slashing of a sharp object.

Besides where they had entered, there were only two other doors in the hallway. The one to the side led into another room. Its door was open. The door at the end of the hallway led outside to a set of stairs. The outside door was propped open.

"How many do you think there are?" one of the guards asked.

"There's only one," the commander replied, "a female, a very dangerous female. Stay alert."

"One Featral did all of this?"

"Secure the room," the commander ordered, indicating half of the group. They responded by moving cautiously through the open side door.

The commander took the rest of the party down the hall, scanning the bodies as they passed.

He lowered his weapons slightly. "Looks like she's already outside." He reported their findings over the comms. "We have a runner. Looks like she escaped and left a trail of bodies behind her."

"She must not get away," a voice bellowed in reply. "We're sending aerial reinforcements to the facility to help search and terminate her. She's dangerous. Pull out to safety. We'll take over from here."

"Roger." The commander nodded to those with him and then spoke over the comms again. "Let's get out of here. Reinforcements are on the way and will handle it."

"Roger," a voice crackled from inside the room. "There's nothing in here but a few more dead and some infant Featral corpses.

As one guard emerged from the room, he suddenly turned back toward it. "What the…"

"Look out!"

"Argh!"

A light flashed, and the sound of a laser blast jumbled in with the continuing background cry of the sirens.

The guard's body jerked back through the doorway and out into the hall, where he collapsed to the floor.

Before the commander could point his laser, a shadow bounced off the opposite wall, firing off shots that dropped the remaining two guards by his side.

The commander fired at the rolling shadow but missed.

The shadow didn't. The commander's body crashed against the wall and slid to the floor.

The shadowy figure was a Featral woman. Using the light from her laser, she checked beneath the bundle tied securely across her chest using strips of cloth. It was a Featral infant.

The infant didn't respond to the light, his blue eyes staring lethargically at her.

She touched his curly blue hair, and the infant closed his eyes in response.

The woman's stringy blue hair was shaved on the right side of her head, exposing a fresh curved scar that extended from the top of her head down below her left cheekbone. Her eye was made of cybernetic aluminum and was not functional. A flesh-covered patch covered the back of her neck where her Bohmian device had been removed days prior.

She shivered involuntarily, then blinked to ward off the effects of the drugs that were meant to subdue her.

She turned off the light and covered the infant again. Then she ran down the hallway, jumping over bodies as she went.

Once outside, she took leaping strides up the stairs, pausing when she reached the top. The frigid night air swiped a gush of wind across her body. Even though the infant was already strapped tightly to her, she instinctively held him closer to her side. She could hear the continued blasting of the sirens in the night. She knew the grounds would soon be covered with soldiers.

Sixty feet away, a group of four soldiers rushed by on their way to board small search vehicles parked to the side. She crouched so as not to be discovered. However, it was too late. One of the soldiers spotted her and yelled to the others.

Before he could draw his weapon, she let shots fly. His body jerked back and flung to the ground. The others opened fire as she ran parallel to their position toward some trees. Another soldier fell. The other two rushed toward the protection of their flight vehicles.

The Featral female noted their decision and changed course, running directly toward them. She shot the third in the back. The soldier fell face first, his body sliding to a stop within inches of the vehicle.

The final soldier managed to open his craft and attempted to enter. A laser shot scorched the back of his head, followed by multiple shots to his back. He fell over, partially hanging into the craft. When she reached him, she yanked him onto the ground. His body flopped onto it back, his arm falling to the side. She fired several shots to sever his forearm. Then she holstered her weapon, grabbed his forearm, and jumped into the driver's seat.

"Ignition!" she shouted, "Manual override."

"Voice recognition does not compute for this vehicle."

"Scanner." The center divider opened, revealing a hand scanner. She put the soldier's hand on it and repeated the order along with a security code she had stolen.

She watched impatiently as the light blinked while it computed the information. Then the engine vibrated to life.

"Manual override is complete. You may proceed."

She directed the craft to rise and then flew off into the night sky.

Several shots flew past her, fired by some robots that had arrived on the scene. Three of the robots entered the remaining craft to give chase.

She kept the craft at a low trajectory, checking the holographic guidance system to get her to the freeway grid. Using the manual override, she hoped to blend in with the other craft. However, she knew her chances were slim. She was sure the escaping craft had been reported.

She took a moment to loosen her grip on the infant. She uncovered him, and the infant's eyes opened slightly as he tried to focus on her. He clutched the cloth in front of him, taking short quick breaths.

"Hang in there, little one," she said, rocking him slightly. Then she covered him again.

She was interrupted by the vehicle's computer. "The 210 grid is approaching. Please reduce speed to enter the grid."

"Confirm reduction of speed to allow grid entrance mark three, two, one, mark." She allowed the craft's manual controls to link to the grid. As she did, she noted on her hologram three approaching craft closing the gap between them from a distance. She tried desperately to mangle the signals with a generic identity to camouflage the vehicle's mark upon its entrance. However, she wasn't sure if she was successful.

She locked into a lane and a level and then flew at the designated speed so as not to draw more attention to herself. It was then fighters entered her radar and flew over her space. A twinge of panic reverberated through her body, not for her sake but for the infant. She unraveled him to look at him again. This time, the hand that had clutched the cloth before plopped lifelessly to his side. His eyes were motionless, and he was no longer gasping for air.

She clutched the infant to her side, squeezing her eyes shut as tears rolled down her cheeks. Just then, the other vehicles on the grid were simultaneously moved to the side of the freeway away from her vehicle. She had no control. Feeling numb, she gazed at the image on the hologram that showed one of the fighters releasing its missile. Within seconds, her fate would be the same as the child within her grasp. She closed her eyes.

◆———◆———◆

The phone intercom was answered, and a voice at the other end spoke. "The subject and the infant she stole have been terminated."

"Thank you for the news, Captain Rubik. This is very unfortunate. How many did we lose?"

"Four scientists and fifteen soldiers, sir."

"That's more than the last time," Rubik responded with a sigh. "Please make the standard family notifications and arrangements."

"Yes, sir."

"She was next to impossible to control. Tell the troops they have done their duty."

"Yes, sir."

"It's been a long, stressful night. If it isn't one thing it's another. Thank God someone invented coffee." He chuckled. "Oh well, I have a very important meeting in the morning. Those Mandarin bastards have attacked one of our main facilities. They're getting smarter, but we'll get them."

"Yes, sir, we'll get them."

"Try to get some sleep. Goodnight, Captain."

"Goodnight, sir."

BACK IN HOUSTON

The hallway was long. The time was 0855. Quentarius, Socrates, and Ton walked briskly in formal black military dress. Quentarius led the way, Socrates and Ton walking behind him on either side. The sound of their shoes echoed to the sequence of their strides. Their gait was serious, their expressions stoic. They knew they were about to be assigned to a mission of great difficulty.

The Featral formal military outfits were not as rigid looking like the norm, but they were formal, nonetheless. Everything was black except for their royal-blue collars, which matched their blue hair and eyes.

They approached non-Featral military guards standing on both sides of two large mahogany doors. The doors were open. Quentarius led Socrates and Ton into a large conference room. The Featral didn't acknowledge the guards, nor did the guards bother to stand at attention to acknowledge them. The guards closed the doors behind them.

The room resembled a holographic war room. Images floated above a large conference table. Standing around the table was a general in full uniform and Captain Johnson. There was also an older Caucasian man in a black suit. He stood with his back to them in the corner. The scent of freshly brewed coffee permeated the room. The man in the suit poured himself a cup.

Captain Johnson greeted them. "Ah, Quentarius. I believe you know everybody here. Socrates, Ton, this is General Newton, and the gentleman over there is Mr. Benjamin Gascon from the Gamble Corporation. They exchanged nods. Mr. Gascon didn't turn around.

They all waited a few moments while Mr. Gascon finished doctoring his coffee. Finally, he turned, held up his mug to the others, and took a sip. He smiled to himself, pleased with the taste. "Always tastes better when you make a fresh pot yourself the old-fashioned way." He walked over them. "My, my, Socrates, look at you. You've grown strong over the years, and your skills have become second to none. We're extremely pleased with your progress."

Socrates' mind questioned the familiarity this man had regarding him, as Socrates had no recollection of him.

Johnson held out his hand for them to sit.

"And the battle-tested and most excellent Quentarius," Mr. Gascon continued. "How are you feeling these days?"

"Fine, sir. Thank you."

"Wonderful." Mr. Gascon turned his attention back to Socrates and Ton. "We offer our condolences for the unnecessary termination of one of your team members. Please know that the outlandish behavior of Dr. Snider and Mr. Humphrey is not a reflection of the Gamble Corporation's objectives in preparing troops for battle." Mr. Gascon waved his hand in the air nonchalantly. "We thank you for saving us the time and expense with your administration of justice in this situation." He paused and took another sip of coffee. "That Featral was a good soldier. It's too bad. We could have used her on this mission." He pointed at the general. "But I'll let General Newton and the captain here fill you in on the details."

Johnson leaned over and maneuvered a couple of holographic images in front of them, then locked in the view he wanted. It was an image of a large Gamble Corporation compound. Around it was a dome-shaped force field that extended about 2,900 ft in height. Around the compound and inside the dome, several ground battles were happening at once.

"Command zoom out at four."

The image zoomed out for a broader view. They saw there were battles outside of the dome as well, including air strikes. Johnson maneuvered the image and enlarged it over the conference table. The image slowly rotated as Socrates and the others took in the vision.

"What you see is a strategically important compound that was guarded by non-Featral security," General Newton said. "Compounds like this are where much of our advanced military technology and secrets are housed. About two days ago, the Mandarins discovered the compound and laid siege to it. Their objective appears to be to possess and confiscate. You can imagine what will happen if they succeed. We cannot let that happen. That's why we're planning a special ops mission. We believe your team can pull it off."

He paused for effect.

"After the Mandarin siege commenced, we deployed our nearest troops to aid the compound. In the escalation, we sent for combined Featral and military forces to be dispatched. However, before this intervention, we were cut off by this advanced technology." He pointed to the force field. "It's a different kind of force field, as you can see. Those who are inside cannot get out, and those who are outside cannot get in. We're fighting them off inside the dome and fighting them outside of the dome. They are slowly winning the battle inside, and it appears they will eventually possess the compound for however long they need to transfer information and confiscate what they want."

"Do we know how they were able to create such a large force field?" Quentarius asked. "Is there a field core there?"

Newton nodded to Johnson to respond.

"No. There isn't a field core that we can detect. We have not discovered exactly how they did it yet, but we have figured out how to deactivate it. We have experimented before with this kind of technology. Obviously, they are a step ahead of us with the creation of the force field. Show the markers," he commanded. Red lights began to blink on the holographic image. "Our satellites have detected six field markers all within the dome. All six need to be deactivated for the force field to collapse. If one is taken out, another will compensate for the loss. We need to deactivate all six. They can be deactivated by direct contact with an encrypted magnetic device, which we have programmed the codes into, of course. We need special ops to get inside, fight off the enemy forces, deactivate the force field, then secure the perimeter of the compound until our outside armies can take over."

Socrates could see where this was going, various high-risk scenarios running through his mind.

Ton whispered to Socrates and pointed out something, which Socrates acknowledged with a nod.

Quentarius pointed to the force field. "I take it burrowing deep underneath is not an option. It would be too slow and easily detected. And from what you're saying, we need to get our encrypted magnetic devices inside to deactivate the force field."

"Excellent deductions, Quentarius," Newton replied.

"Then what's the plan to get inside?" Quentarius asked.

"You see how smart they are, General?" Mr. Gascon said.

Newton nodded. "Yes, very perceptive."

"Does the small discoloration on top of the dome mean something?" Ton asked.

Newton smiled. "You Featral are always a few steps ahead, aren't you? Captain Johnson, please proceed."

"Top of field ninety-degrees zoom in, three," Johnson commanded. The image zoomed in and rotated sideways, highlighting the discolored area on top of the dome. "We have been monitoring the force field. Every hour there is a barely detectable but complete break in the force field. It appears this is a means for the force field to recalibrate itself. However, when this occurs, there is an opening in the force field here." As he spoke, the circle blinked to highlight the area he was referring to. "The opening remains open for 15.5 seconds before it abruptly closes again. It's large enough for a craft as large as the F-S9 Siren to enter. The margin of error for such a craft is 31.57 feet in width. And the approach must be straight down." He demonstrated with a downward hand gesture.

The Featral exchanged glances.

"Socrates and his team will be the cargo in the F-S9," Johnson continued. "The craft will be loaded with individual flyers. Meanwhile, we will increase the attack outside the force field. The F-S9 can break off at the appointed time to get to the top of the dome. Once inside the force field, the F-S9 will have to level off, avoid inside fire, and release your team of flyers to their destinations to deactivate the markers."

He turned his attention to Quentarius. "Your Featral armies will join our troops on the outside offensive. Once the force field is down, the Featral armies will finish off the battle and prepare a path for our troops to enter and secure the compound."

"If the pilot can't do this, they'll be incinerated by the collision of the force field," Quentarius replied.

"Or the ground," Ton whispered to Socrates.

Socrates smirked as he continued to study the images.

"Most of our pilots cannot be trusted to maneuver the F-S9 and pull this off," Johnson said. "However, we have two Featral pilots here who we believe can."

"Only two?" Socrates replied.

"Who are they?" Quentarius asked.

"Display pilots," Johnson ordered.

Two small images appeared in front of them.

"FFP39431, who goes by the name Tarridine, and FFP40532, who goes by the name Leanna," Johnson said.

Ton looked at Socrates and smirked. Socrates kept his gaze forward.

"You're showing us two," Quentarius said, "but you haven't analyzed which of the two pilots are proper for this mission?"

"We have," Johnson said. "Tarridine will be able to maneuver the plane perfectly. Leanna can too. She seems to adjust to the unexpected a little better, but..." his voice trailed off.

"She takes too many risks," Newton said. "We only have a short window of time and space. Her ad libbing up there could be dangerous."

"Or exactly what we need," Mr. Gascon interjected.

"We can't afford mistakes," Newton said.

Quentarius raised a brow. "The plane may come under attack, both on the outside and on the inside. The pilot will have to adjust to the circumstances and still execute the plan."

"What about missiles?" Socrates asked.

Newton and Johnson glanced at each other and at Mr. Gascon. "We had this very conversation before your arrival," Gascon explained.

"Well, I'm not sold on her," Newton said. "But I'll go along with it. If it doesn't work, the compound's detonations will commence. We'll lose so much work."

"We'll blow the place up rather than allow the enemy to get their hands on what's inside," Gascon said. "So, do you concur?"

Newton and Johnson deferred to each other and then nodded.

"Then I guess it's settled," Newton said. "We'll brief the squadron regarding the plans and prepare the craft. Quentarius, mobilize your forces. You will join the battle in four hours."

The Featral nodded in reply. Then they stood up and headed out.

"And Socrates," Gascon called out after them, "it was really good to see you."

Socrates stopped and acknowledged him. Then he turned and continued out.

✦━━✦━━✦

As they left the room, Mr. Gascon rubbed his hands together with pleasure. "He's better than I could have imagined. Over time, his adaptations to the changes of the gene have paid off. Our scientists will use the blood samples we've collected from him earlier to improve upon the TS solution."

Johnson gave Gascon an inquisitive look. "Sir, Socrates has been exposed differently?"

"Yes. Differently but the same as the other twenty-six. He and the twenty-six others were the highest adaptable subjects to the TS variations. We pushed it further with our experimentation. Unfortunately, the other twenty-six are dead. Besides Socrates, the last of the group was terminated last night. Most of them died within a couple of years. The experiments were scrapped many years ago. But Socrates was one of two who lived on. We've had our eye on him over the last ten years. It seems his body has adapted to the gene's mutations."

"We've just been given authority to garnish a more powerful solution," Newton said. "We'll start testing it with the next batch of fetuses."

"I knew there was something special about Socrates," Johnson remarked.

"Indeed, there is, Captain," Gascon replied.

"Then I'll leave to make arrangements." Johnson stood up and saluted. "Good day, General. Mr. Gascon."

Newton returned the salute. Mr. Gascon nodded his approval. "Good luck, Captain."

Johnson left to make the necessary preparations.

<hr />

After leaving the meeting, the three Featral walked down the hall the same way they had come in, all of them silent.

Ton waited until they were outside before finally turning to Socrates. "How can we be sure about this Leanna, L1?"

"We'll know shortly if it was the right choice or not, L2. Choices are made, and we live with the consequences. Death is inevitable."

"Yes, but I'd rather die fighting than be taken down as a passenger on a plane. And they never said what will happen to her or the plane once we're released inside."

"They are not concerned about what she does once the force field is deactivated," Quentarius said.

"We'll have to figure it out. Don't be surprised by their treachery."

"Dr. Snider reminded us of that fact," Ton replied.

"What they did to your team is not an isolated event," Quentarius said. "But something else doesn't sit well with me. Why don't they want Featral to secure the compound?"

"Yes, I caught that," Socrates agreed.

Just then, Quentarius held his side and grimaced.

"Are you alright, sir?" Socrates asked.

"It's nothing to be concerned about. What I am concerned about is that there's something in there they don't want us to see. Our underground hasn't been able to find out what. Remember what I said about us being very resourceful? Well, we have programmers, techs, and the like all around. We also have access to our own intelligence network. We're offering those resources to you."

"We gladly accept any aid you are willing to offer us," Socrates replied.

"Great. I need to prepare my troops, and you need to brief your team. We'll speak again after you get inside the force field."

They exchanged goodbyes and saluted each other. Then Quentarius departed.

Socrates turned to Ton. "For the call of duty, we will fight and deactivate this field. The compound will be secure. But we also must cover our team. They have presented their plan, which we will execute. We also need to have a plan of our own. Do you understand, L2?"

"Yes, L1, clearly."

"Then come. We only have a few hours."

THE ENTRY

I N THE ONGOING race for air supremacy, the F-S9 Siren was the latest in WAEU fighter craft technology. Historically, as soon as a fighter craft was developed, it would be short lived, the opposition responding with a better model to offset the original. However, this constant tactical race for supremacy had been somewhat stalemated for years. The WAEU's focus was on developing better pilots, Featral pilots.

Featral pilots were linked to the technical equipment by the Bohmian devices. They were better able to handle the increased Mach speeds and thrust-vectoring technology in the modern craft. The development of the laser cannon to complement conventional armaments also worked in their favor. The WAEU had tactical superiority when faced with the inferior Mandarin fighters.

Leanna inspected the inside of the F-S9 with great satisfaction. Meanwhile, ground personnel fueled the craft and did final checks. Just inside the craft's narrow cabin, six flyers locked into place. The flyers were facing forward, paired together in twos. To either side were passenger seats facing inward. This was where Socrates' team would sit. There was only one seat in the cockpit, Leanna's seat. It seemed to her that everything was in order.

When Leanna received the assignment, she almost leaped with delight. She had been recognized for her skill and considered worthy of pairing up with special ops. It wasn't just the assignment per se; she would also have the opportunity to pair up with Socrates Challenge. She hoped she would make a better impression than she had previously.

Captain Johnson had briefed her in detail about the mission. She had to be prepared for any contingency that presented itself. Leanna was a skilled pilot, and the sky was her domain. She was confident in her abilities. Her esteemed passengers would not distract her.

She sat in the cockpit and gave the controls a final once-over. She glanced out the window and observed Socrates and his team approaching. They were wearing their customary fitted black armored uniforms. Each had a small backpack. With them were two other ground Featral and Captain Johnson. The captain conversed with them as they approached.

Leanna made eye contact with Johnson and gave a casual salute. He nonchalantly returned the gesture. The Featral simply glanced up without response.

Johnson concluded his conversation with them and then departed. Then the Featral boarded the plane.

Leanna came out of the cockpit to greet them, addressing Socrates first. "Good afternoon, sir. Wonderful day for a flight."

"Good afternoon," Socrates responded with a smirk. He introduced the others. They acknowledged her in return. However, the two other Featral who came in with them walked past Leanna during the introductions. They pulled out devices that had been previously hidden, causing Leanna to give them an inquisitive look.

"They're from Quentarius," Socrates said. "They're officially here to ensure the locks are secure on the flyers and that they will be released for our exit according to plan."

Leanna turned and saw that the two were scanning areas of the plane beyond the flyers. There was not much space to maneuver around. They stepped around the flyers as they continued their scan. "I assure you they are secure and will be released as planned," she said.

The two Featral paused and looked at her, then continued as before.

"It's OK," Socrates replied. Just then, one of the Featral's devices beeped.

"We have one," the Featral said. He pushed a button, and a small holographic image appeared, showing from behind one of the plane's panels the image of a strategically placed detonator that could destroy the plane from the inside. The detonator could be activated from another location.

Leanna stared at it, puzzled.

"They do not intend for you to come back after the drop," Ton said, his face serious.

Leanna shook her head. "I don't understand."

Ton gave her an assuring look. Although she felt betrayed, she said no more. Notwithstanding, this gave her an added confidence in who she was flying with. She wasn't flying for the WAEU. She was flying for the Featral and Socrates Challenge.

"Deactivate the detonator, but keep the tracking device activated," Socrates ordered. "There's no point tipping them off that we know about it."

"Deactivate detonator," the Featral said. When he spoke, part of the device broke off. Several spider-type nanobots crawled and melted into a small shaft that led between the plane's panels. The hologram showed the intrusion of the spider bots as they swarmed the detonator. The image flashed.

"Detonator permanently deactivated. Tracking is still functional."

The nanobots returned in like manner and reassembled into the Featral's device. The two Featral who had conducted the scan nodded to each other and then headed out. "All is secure, sir," one of them said.

"I haven't seen such an adapted device like that before," Ton said.

"They don't know we have this," the Featral replied as he concealed the device. "We have 'the special one' working for us. He goes by the name of Triton. This is some of his handiwork." On the way out, they wished the team luck. There was a moment's pause while the two Featral exited the craft.

"So, you've flown the F-S9 before?" Kanga asked.

"Sure, I've flown it many, well a few times."

Socrates smirked at her response. Kanga wasn't amused.

"Does that mean many or few?" she whispered to Ton.

Ton shrugged.

"Don't worry," Leanna said, chuckling. "You're experts on the ground, but I'm the expert in the air. Just activate your helmets, strap in, and enjoy the ride.

We have three minutes until takeoff. When it's time, you'll have to go from your seat to the flyers. I trust you can handle that."

"Yes, I think we can handle it," Socrates replied.

"I'll try to keep her steady when you do. Be assured, I'll get you inside the force field, sir," Leanna said as she turned away. "Or we'll all die trying," she added under her breath.

As planned, the team sat near the flyers they would board, three on each side. They confirmed their communication devices were activated and functioning. However, during the flight, they would only be able to communicate with Leanna when she chose to switch frequencies.

Leanna returned to the cockpit, tapping her foot on the floor as she waited. *This is not a drill. This is real.* Finally, she noted it was time. Instead of using the communicator, she turned and shouted back at the others. "OK grounders, they've already kicked these tires! Now let's light these fires!"

The Featral helmets dropped down from above with attached oxygen cords that would be snapped loose when they exited. She signaled for them to put on their helmets, which they did.

Leanna loved what came next. She sat upright in her chair and held her arms out to the sides. "Command startup Foxtrot, Foxtrot, Papa 40532, commence."

Upon her command, a solid black helmet with a tinted visor lowered over her head. Inside was an oxygen mask that pressed to her face. The chinstrap automatically snapped into place, and she instantly felt the probes connect to her head. Within seconds she assumed control of the craft. The engines roared to life.

The craft's computer visibly scanned her body, then digitally began imaging fitted black gloves over her hands. It spread over her body until the holographic suit was complete. Sensors were now embedded all around her within the suit. She was one with the craft. Leanna smiled to herself and shook her head. *I just love this plane.*

A voice crackled into her helmet from air traffic control. "0532, this is Father Nest, do you copy?"

"Your squawk is coming in loud and clear, roger."

"You're cleared for takeoff when ready. Good luck."

"Roger, Father Nest. Where are my blue-haired flying playmates?"

"They'll catch up to you. We have not received word that all's clear and secure at the fire dome yet. Most of the activity is to the north side to clear the way for grounders."

"Roger. Hopefully, we can sneak in without too much attention."

"A few craft approaching from the south hopefully won't register enough of a threat for any of them to break off. Your approach might just be uneventful."

"All the same, Father Nest, how many are joining us?"

"Two F-35-Sonic M2s."

Leanna paused. "Just two M2s huh?" she said sarcastically. "Roger. Thank command for the outpouring of support."

"Well, like you said, we can't have you drawing too much attention, 0532."

"Roger. Preparing to lift."

Leanna did a final check of the holographic controls. Then she directed the craft to lift. The roar of the engines increased as the plane shuddered and lifted off. The F-S9 was not much for a speedy takeoff. However, once it got going, it was fast and as maneuverable as the smaller M2 fighter craft, especially under Featral control. The F-S9 slowly turned 180 degrees and powered forward, increasing its speed and altitude in the process.

Socrates' body moved in its harness from the sudden change in g-force and forward movement. Kanga looked uncomfortably toward Ton, who returned a slight grin. Kanga had flown before but hadn't been inside a supersonic craft since her early training. They all knew she was not fond of those memories.

Soon, Leanna settled into a nice steady pace. She laughed to herself at the grounders obvious discomfort, although what they would face on land was, in her mind, both terrifying and impossible.

She passed through a light cloud and smiled; her vision outside temporarily obscured. As the blue sky reappeared, she let her mind absorb the peace and tranquility below. The ground and the clouds rushed past. The world was indeed a terrifying place, but at moments like these, she was able to appreciate the magnificence of the dwelling place called Earth. *Such a beautiful place. How did we ever get to the sad state that we're in now?*

Leanna's thoughts were interrupted by the presence of other craft. Two images appeared on her holographic radar screen, her escorts.

"0532, your party playmates for fire dome have arrived," a voice said over her ear link.

"Roger. Please identify."

"Roger. 8789 coming your way."

"Roger. 8789 marked and secured," Leanna replied.

"Good afternoon, Crazy Bird. 9431 is happy to join the party. Ooh wee, I'm coming in with fangs out."

Leanna smiled to herself, knowing there was only one person who called her "Crazy Bird."

"9431 marked and secured. Welcome to the party, Tarridine. Hopefully, we won't have much activity outside of the fire dome, but I'm glad you can make it."

"Roger. I wouldn't miss it," Tarridine replied.

"Let's keep our scans expanded out for those wanting to crash our party," Leanna said.

"Roger," 8789 said.

"Roger. Head is on a swivel," Tarridine replied.

The two M2s caught up and matched Leanna's pace on both sides of her craft. Even though the F-S9 was not a large craft, it appeared to be in comparison to the two fighters. As she viewed Tarridine's craft, he gave her a two-fingered salute. She smiled and saluted back, then mentally directed the craft into a 360-degree spin. It was a normal maneuver done during their training to signal they were ready for a fight. The M2s returned the gesture, twisting their planes repeatedly in the late-afternoon sky.

Leanna was already confident but having Tarridine with her encouraged her even more. He was the one pilot whom she felt she could still learn from, and now she was going into battle with the best covering possible. She had Tarridine by air and Socrates Challenge's team on the ground.

Just then she remembered that maybe she should have given her passengers some warning before she twirled. Using a mere thought and a twitch of her eye, Leanna switched her frequency to communicate with her passengers. "Sorry for the sudden movement. How are you doing back there, sir?"

"Everything is fine back here," Socrates replied.

"I think Kanga doesn't feel well," another Featral joked.

"That's not funny," Kanga said. "Can you at least let us know when you're going to do that next time?"

"Will do," Leanna replied. "I need to remember you grounders aren't used to the sudden movements of high-speed flight. But you do remember our approach will be straight down, right?"

"Yes," Kanga replied unenthusiastically.

"How long until we get there?" Socrates asked.

"Thirteen minutes and twenty seconds until the opening in the force field. When the red light comes on, it'll be time to mount the flyers."

"Roger."

She switched her frequency back and continued flying. The target had just entered Leanna's holographic radar space. She knew the enemy had them in view as well. It was just a question if they would respond and how. The enemy's combat fighters were not drones, nor were they manned by robots. They were manned by human pilots. They flew as proficiently as humanly possible, but the Featral were able to control their craft even faster.

The sun reflected through the partial clouds, but something wasn't right. Leanna could feel tension building. The sky seemed to pause with the anticipation of potential violence. Suddenly, a crackling sound came into her ear.

"Six bandits coming straight at us with mal intent. Crazy Bird, you see them?"

"Roger. Prepare for evasive maneuvers."

Leanna noted the six fighters on the hologram. They were lined straight across and were headed directly toward them. "We don't want them to get a clear lock on us. It looks like we're having a dogfight after all. What's your pleasure, Tarridine?"

"Initiating blink. Let's go evasive breakpoint eight on my mark, Crazy Bird."

"Roger," Leanna replied.

"8789, Roger," the other M2 pilot.

At that, the two M2s increased their speed to get out in front and create space. Leanna slightly decreased hers. Soon they would be locked with enemy fighters in a continued state of motion, evading and exchanging laser fire.

Leanna switched the communication frequency to her passengers. "We have six hostiles approaching. Brace yourselves. It's going to be a rough ride."

       •———•———•

Kanga glanced anxiously at Ton, then turned her head and closed her eyes.

Socrates felt the thrill of battle. However, this time he had to depend on this Featral fighter pilot. They had to trust her. There was no choice.

       •———•———•

The Featral's vision and accuracy from a great distance were far superior. Their M2s would fire first and capitalize on that advantage. As the M2s darted into a patch of clouds, rapid beams of fire blurred into the atmosphere. Five seconds went by before the approaching planes reacted and broke their formation. It was too late for one of them. A ball of flame ignited, and a stream of black smoke trailed behind it. The others returned fire.

A few opposition planes jumped altitude. Tarridine spun his M2 sideways to avoid fire. Then he climbed to join them. As he did, Tarridine fired at the underbelly of another, avoiding more fire at the same time. The enemy plane exploded.

The M2s and the F-S9 were now in constant motion—up and down to one side and then the other. Leanna was fully engaged from behind them. She smiled to herself as another enemy plane went down. It was now a three-on-three battle.

The planes were suddenly upon each other. With blinding speed, they crossed each other's paths at differing elevations and angles. Both groups started to circle back to reengage. However, Leanna kept flying straight toward the force field. When one of the enemy planes passed her going the opposite direction, it released two heat-tracking missiles before it started to circle back.

The missiles immediately appeared on her screen. "Heaters!" Leanna exclaimed. "Two of them!"

"Roger. Coming back around," 8789 replied.

"Hang on," Tarridine interjected. "I'm still on a bandit." He was already at the higher altitude with the highest enemy plane. When he circled around, the other hadn't yet completed his turn. Tarridine increased his angle of attack, locked in, and started to fire. The plane twisted and dove, avoiding the hit. Tarridine repositioned himself to maintain the advantage.

"This guy is good," he said over the comms. "I'll break off when I can. I have a tiger up here."

Meanwhile, the other M2 came in hard behind Leanna, trailing the missiles. Lana had released reflectors to try to distract the missiles, but the missiles flew right through and didn't respond to them. Leanna turned and dove to the right. The missiles followed. Leanna turned abruptly the other direction while straightening her plane out with a 360 twist. This caused the missiles to hesitate for a second before they changed their trajectory back to Leanna's path. The maneuver bought her some additional separation though. Leanna continued to maneuver but didn't deviate from the general direction of the approaching force field.

The M2 closed in behind the missiles and locked in.

The other two enemy planes were also some distance behind trying to get in position behind them both.

The M2 fired at one of the missiles. It exploded into a haze of flames. The M2 readjusted to get back into alignment with the next missile that constantly changed its path with Leanna's maneuvers. As the M2 fired at the remaining missile, the other planes fired on him. The M2 twisted to avoid the aggressive fire streams flying past him. At the same time, due to his own fire, the missile exploded in front of him.

Seconds later, eight new missiles entered the fray from behind, four from each of the trailing planes. The missiles dropped and ignited with aggressive flashes toward the Featral fighters. The M2 and Leanna were the prey.

"Two planes and more heaters!" the Featral pilot reported.

"Divide and crisscross our paths!" Leanna shouted. "Divide and cross!"

"Roger!"

I'm losing time, Leanna thought. *I need to get to the force field. What's keeping Tarridine?*

◆———◆———◆

Tarridine was intertwined in a high-speed, twisting air chase with the lone plane. He had to continue to adjust with precision behind it to maintain his advantage. The enemy plane turned aggressively away from Tarridine's constant fire. With his superior Featral skill and accuracy, Tarridine knew he should have already disposed of the fighter. However, the pilot was better than anyone he had encountered, beyond the realm of any non-Featral pilot, robot, or drone. Nevertheless, he didn't have a moment to ponder it. Every few seconds was accompanied with a series of abrupt moves and counter moves. Tarridine still had the advantage, and he was not going to relinquish it.

Finally, Tarridine predicted one of the fighter's maneuvers enough to fire his lasers into its cockpit. The following seconds were followed by more shots that connected with the plane. It burst into streams of fire and fell into a dive, black smoke trailing behind it. The pilot ejected.

Tarridine flew past in a furious blur. In doing so, he lost track of the ejected pilot. Finally, he turned and roared toward the force field to join the rest of the action.

+——+——+

The M2 and Leanna weaved back and forth, the force field now off to Leanna's right. She noted the time and commanded an audible count every thirty seconds beginning at five minutes. It was already 4:29 until the opening. Now she realized she would get there too quickly. She would have to bide some time.

Six of the missiles went with the other M2. Two continued on track toward Leanna's turning plane. The M2 pilot engaged in evasive maneuvers. As he did, he tried to come back around to cross in behind Leanna's path. The remaining enemy planes opened laser fire on the M2. Leanna's plane was near to crossing in front of him and the missiles trailing her. The second she flew by, the M2 took out the two missiles and attempted an evasive dive. Leanna knew he was in trouble.

Laser fire clipped the M2's wing, causing the plane to jerk in such a way that it was hit by the missiles. It was too late to eject. The missiles obliterated the fighter. Two other missiles hesitated and twirled, then readjusted back to Leanna's trail. The last one was damaged and sputtered downward, crashing below.

Leanna felt a rush of sadness for the downed Featral. However, she had to maintain her focus.

Suddenly, one of the two planes who were behind the M2 was hit by the shots from above and burst into flames. Tarridine was back into the fray. He had caught up to them and was barreling down with fury. The remaining enemy plane immediately broke away from

Tarridine's approach and away from Leanna. Tarridine went after it.

"Four minutes," the voice inside Leanna's plane said.

She now had some comfortable separation from the remaining two missiles. However, she knew that gap would close again. She barreled ahead toward the force field.

"Three minutes and thirty seconds."

Despite the g-force, she switched frequencies to talk to her passengers. "Sorry Challenge, but I'm not going to be able to slow down and steady. Get ready to board the flyers." She switched frequencies again.

Socrates and the others readied themselves. Soon they would be either in the middle of a battlefield or die in the sky. They peered at the bulb in the corner. No one moved or said a word as the plane continued to jerk in one direction and then another.

"Flash@" the light screamed. Featral harnesses and straps were released. Moving against the resistance of the g-force, they went to board their flyers. Leanna had to maneuver once again, unexpectedly diving and spinning. A few of the Featral had yet to secure themselves and almost flew off. Kanga barely hung on. Her feet flew in the air as her right hand gripped the flyer for dear life. The plane jerked back, and Kanga's body slammed back into the flyer. She forced herself onto it and then locked her feet into place.

It didn't take long for Tarridine to dispatch the final enemy plane. However, it was long enough to separate him away once again from Leanna and the remaining missiles.

"Two minutes and thirty seconds."

Leanna now was over the force field. Below her, machinery and military personnel were engaged in battle. Laser streams and combustible outbursts ignited the activity inside the force field.

Meanwhile, the two remaining missiles following her were closing in.

"Two minutes."

Leanna switched her communication back to Tarridine. "Tarridine, the time just hit two minutes! My fun meter is really pegged. I can't break away from these heaters! Can you get a shot in?"

There was an uncomfortable silence. "Negative, Crazy Bird. I'm afraid I can't get there in time. You're on your own, but if I can get a shot off, I will."

"Roger." Leanna ground her teeth together as she continued to twist and turn the plane. Each turn caused the missiles to hesitate, creating space. However, she could not shake them. Leanna was running out of time. The mission necessitated she soon get into position for her direct descent. She had been in tough scenarios during flight-simulation training. However, this was real. The missiles were closing in while the force field beckoned her below.

"One minute and thirty seconds until the force field opens."

Leanna's mind quickly deduced the situation. She calibrated the holographic image of the force field and determined measurements of time and space, all within seconds. Then she jerked the plane downward toward the force field's edge. The two missiles plummeted with her.

"One minute until the force field opens."

Her craft leveled over the top part of the force field, flying within inches along the slight curvature of the dome, hoping the missiles would slam into the force field when she did. However, they continued to close in aggressively behind her. The tip of one of her wings started to glow red hot from the plane's speed and the force field's closeness to it.

"Thirty seconds until the force field opens," the voice announced. The countdown could now be heard throughout the plane. Socrates and his team clutched onto the flyers. Their fate would be determined in less than a minute.

Leanna jerked the plane up and away from the force field and then back down again. The missiles followed her path. When they did, one of the missiles came down on the force field and exploded. The second was knocked off its course and sputtered up and away.

"Seventeen, sixteen, fifteen.."

Leanna broke away and ascended toward the middle of the dome. The sputtering missile locked back on the plane and started toward it.

"Ten, nine, eight, seven…"

Considering the timing, Leanna reached a peak above where the opening would occur and reversed her engines to allow the plane to fall straight down.

"Three, two, one, opened." The reverse countdown for the closing of the force field commenced.

She regained forward control and descended straight down.

The missile recalibrated and dove in behind her.

She could see the opening on her hologram. She also noted the missile behind her.

The reverse countdown continued. "Ten, nine, eight, seven..."

Intensity increased as she barreled downward, the small opening rapidly drawing closer.

The missile narrowed the gap between them.

She squinted and forced a spurt from her thrusters. In her mind, everything became silent.

"Three, two..."

In the blur of a split second, the plane erupted through the opening.

The missile above exploded, raining fire and debris onto the closing force field.

However, she was coming in too fast. She partially reversed the engines and tried to level the front of the plane before it collided with the ground. They had entered a war zone. She maintained her intense focus as the plane's nose started to level out.

"Come on!" she exclaimed. "Come on!"

The plane finally leveled just before it collided with the ground, though it scraped along the surface. In the process, it collided with several unprepared Mandarin ground bots. Laser shots flew past the plane, one of them piercing its wing. She signaled for the release of Socrates and his team.

◆————◆————◆

The oxygen connections snapped loose. The door lowered. Two by two, the flyers were released. The flyers' sudden intrusion into the battle caused the enemy Mandarin bots to turn their focus on them. The Featral flyers returned fire and then split up, heading toward their predetermined destinations.

By this time, Leanna's craft had been hit several times, the bombardment of enemy rounds disrupting the craft's basic functioning. She struggled for control but knew it was no use. She steered the plane toward a squadron of enemy tanks, planning to crash it into them.

I must eject.

Once she ejected, with all the laser shots and cannon blasts around, she couldn't release her chute too soon, or she would not survive the trip to the ground. She would merely be a slowly descending target. She decided on a forward-moving free fall. Getting as close to the ground as possible before releasing the chute was her best chance for survival. She could only hope she would not break any limbs or perish in the process.

Noting the distressed craft, Socrates diverted his flyer toward it. Another Featral, L4, followed.

Leanna pulled the eject lever. The cockpit flew open, Leanna's body was compressed into the chair, and she was propelled out into the chaos. Her holographic suit disappeared, except for the helmet and the cushioned, armored shell that surrounded her body.

The abandoned plane crashed into the squadron of tanks, creating a fiery inferno of damage.

Streams of laser fire whiz past her. At the peak of its arc, the chair separated from her. Sixty feet in the air, she and the chair tumbled forward and downward.

Leanna lost her sense of direction, but she had to take her chances. She released the chute. It expanded behind her, abruptly halting her forward momentum. She grunted as the straps yanked her body back with unforgiving force. As she swung downward and forward toward the fast-approaching ground, laser blasts burned through her chute.

The Featral flyers covered her with their own fire as much as they could. Bots collapsed from the impact of their streaming laser fire.

Leanna had slowed considerably, but she was still racing forward. Not wanting to entangle herself in the chute, she hit the device above her chest and released the chute right before she hit the ground. When she hit, she let out another painful grunt. She bounced and rolled in a cloud of dust. The armored shell protected her from the initial impact but faded away as she bounced forward. She bit into her lower lip as the wind was knocked out of her, finally sliding to a rough stop on her back.

Feeling disoriented, instinct forced her to raise her head. She felt a sharp pain to her side and struggled to regain control of her breath. Leanna tasted the metallic taste of her own blood, which had formed on her lip upon impact. She also felt the sting of the exposed flesh on her arms, legs, and torso, her clothing ripped.

Feeling fortunate to be alive, she tried to get her bearings. Through her helmet's dirty face shield, she saw Socrates heading for her, firing shots as he approached. Socrates himself was being covered by L4's flyer.

With all her strength, Leanna forced herself up and held her arm out toward Socrates.

Socrates extended his arm and slowed enough to scoop her up. Their arms locked, and Leanna twisted her body and pulled herself up behind him onto the flyer. She cried out at the newly discovered pain she felt from her elbow and knee. However, she locked her feet in and clutched onto him. The flyer picked up speed and altitude. Socrates again retrieved his gun and shot at another bot as they jetted by. Socrates maneuvered away from the explosions of plane debris and flew up and away in haste.

Seeing Leanna secure and away on Socrates' flyer, L4 turned abruptly and flew off in the opposite direction. The Featral headed to his own designated location to deactivate his section of the force field.

Kanga flew to where her tracking system led her. She was fortunate there was only limited fighting where she was. For the moment it was a pocket area that was void of enemy combat. Her marked and familiar flyer didn't cause the friendly forces to react against her.

She set her gaze on the barrel-size metal rod that stuck out three feet above the ground. The target had been found. She lowered the flyer and circled back. Kanga reached for her pouch and retrieved the device given to her at the beginning of the mission. When she passed by the target, she tossed the device toward the rod. It magnetically guided itself downward and attached itself to the side of the rod. A light flashed from the device, and spider-like legs came out from the device and crawled up to the top. Once there, the legs retracted, and the device started to digitally decode it.

Kanga circled around it once again looking to set the flyer down. After the harsh plane ride, she was eager to place her feet on solid ground. Feeling it was safe to land for a moment, she halted the flyer next to the rod and examined the device. It continued to blink a steady rhythm, signaling that the decoding was still in process. Finally, the device stopped blinking, and the top of the rod opened.

Just then a brigade of friendly non-Featral foot soldiers passed by on their way to a skirmish. A few paused to look at what Kanga was doing. She acknowledged them with a nod, then climbed off her flyer and walked to the opened rod. She drew her laser gun and shot several shots inside, deactivating the rod. There was a slight surge in the force field that was barely noticeable to the human eye. Then the force field recalibrated itself.

Kanga holstered her gun and removed her helmet. Her blue hair stood out in stark contrast to everything else around her. Appreciating the reprieve, Kanga took a long, deep breath of the war-torn air. Some of the soldiers looked at her in wonder.

Kanga activated her headset. "This is L3. My target is out. I'm headed to the safe point."

She didn't get a reply right away. However, eventually, Ton responded over the noise of warfare. "Roger that, L3. This is L2. My target is also out, and I'm heading to the safe point."

"Roger."

Meeting together at a designated safe point was outside the plans of Captain Johnson's knowledge. Thanks to Quentarius's contact, Triton, it was revealed an intentionally secluded entrance point that led inside the Gamble Corporation's facility. It went beneath the protective field.

The other three Featral came in and confirmed deactivation. However, Socrates had yet to confirm. Kanga had lost track of him when the flyers exited the plane. *Socrates is probably OK. He's always OK,* she told herself, disregarding her initial thoughts of concern.

On the other hand, she was unsure about the fate of their pilot. It was clear that the pilot had done her job, and Kanga had done hers. Now Kanga needed to go where she had been ordered to be. She climbed back onto her flyer and put her helmet on. She nodded to the last of the passing brigade, then rose and turned the flyer, jetting off toward the safe point.

◆——◆——◆

Socrates maneuvered through intense fire. Leanna continued to clutch onto him, which limited his movements. He knew she was injured. However, her hold was evidence she was not too weak to continue. To get to the rod, he needed to be on the ground.

He flew over the rod and released his device. It magnetically guided itself downward and attached itself. The device climbed to its place and began to digitally decode the rod.

Socrates connected his communication to Leanna. "Are you alright?"

"I'm in pain but yes."

"Are you able to fly?"

Leanna took a moment to gather herself mentally before responding. "Yes."

"I need to get to the ground. Circle back and get me." Socrates holstered his weapon and descended, slowing down as he did. "On three, let go of me, and grab the controls."

Leanna released her grip on Socrates. "I'm ready."

Socrates continued to fire from the flyer to clear space and create precious seconds. "One, two, three…" He leaped off the flyer and tucked himself into a roll.

Leanna lunged forward and grabbed the flyer's controls. Her ribs screamed in protest at the sharp pain that ripped through her midsection. She ignored it and forced the flyer hard to the right, opening fire upon bots. She disabled one of them and turned again to contest more. This was Leanna's element, and she focused on the job at hand.

Socrates rolled to his feet with laser guns in both hands. He too was in his element. He joined friendly forces around the rod and began attacking Mandarins and Mandarin bots alike. After a short time, the soldiers moved on ahead to where the fighting had advanced. By then the top of the force field rod had opened.

Socrates activated two time-delayed detonators and flung them inside. His adjusted device closed the rod behind them. He opened the communication to Leanna and the team. "L2, we have twenty-seven minutes and fifty seconds on my mark."

"Roger that, L1," Ton replied.

"Now," Socrates said.

"Roger. Marked."

"Leanna, come get me."

"Roger," Leanna replied. "I'm on my way."

She had circled her way back, expecting to reenter the fray when she left him. She was astonished to see Socrates just standing there waiting to get picked up. Bot debris and bodies were all around him, but the fighting had moved to another area.

She landed the flyer next to him, then scooted back to allow him to climb on and take control. "You're very thorough," Leanna said. "But isn't that the last rod? Why is the force field still up?"

"It's on a time delay. They don't care what happens to us after the force field is down. We're going to see what's inside the facility."

"Isn't that against orders?"

"No. After the force field is down, our orders were to allow them to come in and secure the facility. Nothing has changed. The force field will be down in less than thirty minutes. Let's go and join the others."

With Leanna holding on, the flyer powered up from the ground and jetted away.

THE DISCOVERY

a WEAKENING SECOND INNER force field protected the outer shell of the facility. From it, cannon fire launched toward the gathering Mandarin forces coming against it. This was where the core of the battle was concentrated.

Socrates noticed the cannon fire from the facility had a pattern to it. It didn't appear to be efficient. It seemed almost pre-planned and predictable. Socrates led his flyer around the activity toward the safe point.

Waiting for them within a cluster of trees and bushes was his team. Socrates set down the flyer and shut it off. Leanna got off slowly and grimaced as she removed her helmet. Her contortions didn't go unnoticed by the others. Neither did the tattered condition of her torn and bloody uniform. Socrates also removed his helmet and got off.

Ton approached him. "We've confirmed the entrance. It's beneath the ground behind the tree over there," he said, pointing.

"Good. We have no time to lose. According to Triton, this passage will get us inside beneath the facility's inner field. It used to be an old escape route.

Let's get inside before we draw more attention to ourselves."

They nodded and then started to walk over toward the tree.

Leanna grimaced again.

"Where's the plane?" L7 asked.

Leanna shook her head in response.

"We'll not be leaving the way we came," Socrates replied.

"You're injured," Kanga said. "Are you able to continue?"

"I'll be OK," Leanna replied, clutching her side.

Socrates stopped and looked into her eyes. "Are you sure?"

Leanna pressed her lips together and nodded.

Following her assurance, Socrates led them toward the entrance.

Ton and the others had already cleared the vegetation away to expose what amounted to a small manhole. They gathered around it. Ton and L7 grabbed the handles on the cover and pulled. It took some work, but finally it gave way and broke free. They lifted it and set it to the side. A stale, musty stench arose, causing some of them to wince. The opening was only large enough for one person to enter at a time.

"Triton was sure about this, huh?" Kanga said.

Ton smiled and retrieved his laser. He activated his glasses, then he pressed on the light scope from his laser and pointed it down inside. Several bugs scurried away in the face of the light, which illuminated a metal ladder. Dingy steel reflected from the walls and the floor below, signs of rust apparent in spots.

Socrates activated his glasses and then began to descend the ladder. Ton continued to hold the light, so Socrates could see. L7 followed behind Socrates.

The air was stale. Their lights bounced around until Socrates spotted what he was looking for: a small panel on the wall. "Right where Triton said it would be," he said. L7 retrieved a device from his person and magnetically placed it on the panel. After several seconds, fresh air began to filter in. The lights inside flickered and lit up dimly, exposing a tunnel plated with stainless steel. It angled ahead, turning to the right.

The others above activated their glasses and then came down the ladder one by one. Leanna waited to climb down just before Ton, who dragged the cover to close the entrance behind them. Leanna tried to hide her pain, though she climbed down much slower than the rest. Ton waited patiently behind her.

When Ton reached the bottom with the others, he retrieved his own special device and snapped it around his wrist. It projected a small holographic image of the immediate surroundings five inches above his wrist. Ton studied the image as Socrates looked over his shoulder. After several seconds, the guidance system kicked in, displaying their route to access the mainframe.

"This way," Ton said, leading the way. The others drew their weapons and followed him down the passage and around the corner.

Leanna limped along. It was clear she was struggling. However, she had to bear it and keep moving.

Socrates tried to assess why the floors, walls, and ceiling were made of steel. He didn't know why, but he felt a primitive connection with the ambiance of the passage. The reflection of their lights contrasted with the shadows of their black uniforms.

Ton slowed as they approached what appeared to be deactivated robots embedded against individual openings in the wall. The robots were lined up on both sides of the tunnel and were hunched over and immobile, their arms and elongated hands hanging to their sides. Each one was secured to the wall by metal straps.

As they walked by, there was no movement or sound. Socrates felt a cold and desirous emptiness around them as they continued.

Ton scanned one of the immobile bots with his device. It downloaded basic information about the bots. A limited amount of data floated in the air above Ton's wrist. However, it became apparent the complete information could only be retrieved from the mainframe computer. Ton and Socrates sized up the information together.

"HFC F-Series, L224," Ton said. "It's not armed nor programmed for combat. This series was decommissioned a decade ago. They were shipped here for storage."

"What does HFC stand for?" Kanga asked.

"Human Fetus Collector," Socrates replied, looking up from the data. "These are the same type of robots that performed the procedures to save us from being aborted."

They exchanged glances.

"I've never seen one of these before," Leanna said.

"Me neither," Ton replied. "Guess we would have no reason to."

"I have not put much thought into my origin," Leanna said. "Nor have I given much thought about the biological humans who seeded me."

"Why would you?" Kanga replied. "We were taught not to be concerned about it. Besides, it's not important. Achieving of the objective is."

Socrates imagined his biological parents, once again it reminded of his own abandonment. Sure, the Gamble Corporation had stepped in and given him an identity, raised him for a specific purpose. However, the knowledge that there was a deliberate attempt to destroy him before his infancy still stung him. It was the ultimate example of betrayal, a betrayal from the womb, premeditated and deliberate. He wondered if any of humankind could be trusted, including the Gamble Corporation and the military leadership for which he fought. His thoughts were conflicted.

The others noted Socrates' hesitation. He acknowledged them and then gestured for them to push forward. Ton continued to lead the way.

As they passed the robots, Socrates noted that the numbers embedded on their heads descended in numerical order. Odd-numbered robots were on one side, and even-numbered robots were on the other. He counted out the numbers in his head. *F72, F70, F68, F66... F64, F62.*

＊━━━◆━━━＊

The last of the Featral passed by number F66. A faint light from its vision visor flickered. Noting Socrates' DNA, F66 quietly started to activate itself and the others.

The hallway ended just beyond the last robot. At the end of the hallway was a metal door with a digital locking system and a primitive metallic handle beneath the panel. Ton's device continued to direct their way. However, the path led through the door. They gathered around it with one of them keeping an eye behind them toward the stationary robots. Ton changed his settings on the device to unlock the door.

"I think we're being watched," Kanga said, causing the others to ready their weapons.

Suddenly, their attention was drawn down the hall behind them where the sound of breaking metal straps could be heard. That was followed by the hydraulic thuds of robots stepping down into the hallway and trudging toward them. The bots were becoming activated in descending order, from the farthest away down the hall to the closest.

Ton turned his device back at the robots, "Their intentions are unknown."

"Well, I'm not letting them get close enough to ask them," Kanga replied. She took aim and fired at the robots stepping into the passageway. The others joined in reluctantly. The laser fire slowed them but didn't stop them.

"Focus on the door, L2," Socrates said. "Get it open!"

Ton turned back to the door and attached the device to the lock. The tiny light on the device blinked rapidly as it searched for the code.

Meanwhile, the robots continued to be activated down the line. Socrates fired on a robot to try to disable it before it came off the wall. However, he wasn't sure if he succeeded. It became apparent they needed to focus their initial attention on the bots that were already freed.

Each shot made a robot snap back with hesitation. However, then the bots recovered. The Featral quickly discovered it took three to four shots to the head and upper torso to bring them down. But even when one appeared disabled, its legs continued to trudge forward.

As robots began to crumble, other bots tripped over them, causing a pileup. The downed bots attempted to get to their feet, only to be shot down again. Meanwhile, the robots breaking free from the walls surpassed the pile and began climbing down in front of it.

"What's taking so long, L2?" L4 exclaimed.

"I don't like our position, L1!" Kanga shouted. "We're going to have more piles of cyber crap in a minute."

"L2?" Socrates shouted.

Ton gazed coolly at the device as its light continued to blink, seemingly taking its sweet time. "It should be any moment now," Ton replied.

Straps continued to break loose as robots freed themselves. The hydraulic plodding noises intensified.

"Ton?" Socrates asked.

"Any moment."

Robots forced their way through a second pile of fallen bots. More continued to free themselves ahead of them.

The light on the device finally blinked. "Got it," Ton said. He pushed the handle down and forced his shoulder into the door, opening it. He snatched the device and held the door open for the others. "Come on!"

"Go!" Socrates shouted.

They quickly peeled back to escape through the door. Socrates was in the rear. Before he got through, one of the robots got close to him and reached out. Socrates shot its head, causing it to stumble back into another robot. Then he escaped through the door.

Ton slammed it shut behind him. The door automatically locked. Then Ton shot his laser into the door panel to disable it. They heard bots thumping on the door.

<hr />

F66 gathered himself up from one of the piles of cybernetic debris and stood with the remaining bots, glaring at the disabled door.

<hr />

On the other side, Socrates and the others looked around at a sizable warehouse area with three levels. The lighting was dim. Their lights shone in several directions, reflecting off several large storage containers.

Leanna let out a quiet moan of discomfort. She and the others knew there was nothing that could be done for her. Kanga, who was next to Leanna, shone her light on her.

"Are you able to go on?"

"I have no choice."

"Shh…" Ton whispered.

It was then they heard the rhythm of swift, heavy cybernetic footsteps.

"We've got company," Ton said.

Socrates gave Leanna a slight shove, pointing her to get behind a nearby container. Then they turned off their lights and ran off in different directions. Laser fire and sparks immediately lit up the room. Socrates rolled to the opposite side, avoiding a stream of light that had just missed him.

The blasting crunch of laser fire striking metal echoed in the semi-darkness. Fighter bots landed hard on the ground floor, jumping down from the upper levels. When Socrates rolled back to his feet, he fired several shots at nearby bots before they had time to adjust from their landing.

Then, unexpectedly, one of the robots spoke. "Featral," a cybernetic voice said over the melee.

"Featral," another said.

Robots ceased firing and repeated that name throughout the room. After a while, the Featral also ceased firing, although they kept their weapons ready.

"What's going on?" L4 shouted.

A few of their lights began to search their surroundings, reflecting off containers and stationary robots. Ton found the light switch and turned it on.

Kanga found herself several feet from a badly damaged robot that wobbled back and forth repeating the words, "Featral, Featral, Featral…" Kanga stepped up closer and fired two shots into its head. The robot's head jerked back, and it collapsed to the ground.

With both guns still raised, Socrates nodded at Ton to scan the robots. While doing so, Socrates felt a sharp pain in his head. It came from just under his Bohmian device. His eye twitched but he tried to ignore the pain.

Leanna gathered herself from behind the container. They all looked around the room. It was a large warehouse with three levels. It was apparent the area had been recently abandoned. A large opening at the other end was blocked by a huge partition. Standing around were the numerous fighter bots that had attacked them. Far to the left was another door.

Leanna walked up to Ton, who was still working with the device that Triton had given him.

The device quickly revealed the intention of the machines standing around them. The bots were armed but were no longer in attack mode. Ton narrowed his gaze toward Socrates, looked back down at the reading and then back at Socrates again. "L1, are you alright?"

Socrates squinted his left eye and held down his arm. A throbbing sensation rushed to his temple. He fell to one knee and involuntarily trembled, closing his eyes.

"Socrates!" Leanna exclaimed. She started toward him. However, she stopped when the others went back to high alert.

"Socrates," one of the robots said.

"L-1," another robot said, turning its head slightly toward him.

Ton looked up from the data registering from the device and continued to stare at Socrates.

Kanga stiffened her arm and pointed her weapon at the robot closest to her. The others did the same. "What are they doing to him?"

Ton glanced back down at the device and its rapidly moving holographic data. "They're communicating with him."

"Communicating with him?" Leanna said.

Socrates had managed to holster his weapons. He got on his hands and knees and shook his head. The Bohmian device seemed to be pinching him behind his ear. His head continued to throb.

He recalled a time from his youth where he felt the same painful sensations. It was after the device was surgically implanted. He was a young child. As with them all, it was the time when his body adapted to the device. As a child, the pain lasted for days. This was different. It was sharper and more intense.

Socrates heard a variety of digital voices and data rush into his mind all at once. At first it was overwhelming. However, he was eventually able to slow down the information, compartmentalize it, and control it.

Leanna finally stepped closer to him. "Socrates?"

"They are no longer a threat," Ton said.

"Then what are they doing to him?" Kanga asked.

Leanna reached for Socrates' shoulder.

Kanga kept her gun pointed at the bot next to her. "Make them stop."

Gathering himself up to one knee, Socrates patted Leanna's hand to signal he was alright. Over his bombarding thoughts, he was able to speak to his crew. "Ton is correct. There will be no more threats against us from these robots. The humans have already vacated the building. We can proceed to do what we came here to do."

Leanna scrunched her face. "The humans?" she said under her breath.

"It's the Bohmian device," Socrates said, grinning. "I understand their communication. I can feel their communication." Sensing his control over them, Socrates stood. The robots lowered their weapons and then assembled on the ground floor. Socrates' pain rapidly dissipated as control increased. When he finally lifted his head, the robots snapped to attention as one.

The other Featral looked around at each other.

"Are they on our side now?" Leanna asked.

"Looks like it," Kanga replied.

Meanwhile, Socrates picked up on numerous foreign communications he couldn't quite understand. He turned to the door on the far side of him. "Do you hear the chatter?"

L4 looked at him. "Chatter, L1? I can't sense anything besides these bots here."

Socrates nodded to the door. "It's coming from behind there. It's muffled, but it sounds like thousands of nanobots."

Kanga waved her laser at one of the bots. "Ask them."

Ton and L4 approached the door to which Socrates was referring. Ton stopped just short of the door and looked back. "They're definitely nanos but big ones, or maybe small bots. There are a lot of them."

"I'm not sure why we couldn't sense them," the other Featral said. "Maybe it's something in the walls muffling our senses."

Socrates turned from the robot next to him and smirked. Then he walked toward the door, the others following. "The fighter bots are not sure what the nanos are excited about," he said. "These fighters apparently won't communicate with nanos unless they have to, especially these nanos for some reason."

"I wasn't aware there was a class system amongst robots," Kanga replied.

Socrates paused before Ton and locked eyes with him. "It's OK, L2. I have regained control of myself."

"And apparently them too," Kanga remarked as several robots walked to their side.

"What's so special about these nanos to receive such disdain?" Ton asked.

"Let's go see," Socrates replied. He nodded toward one of the bots. It walked up to the door and placed its hand over the scanner, unlocking it. Then the bot stepped away with a hesitation that resembled caution. Socrates put his shoulder against the heavy metal door and pushed it open.

◆——◆——◆

The thundering sound that hit them was like jet engines crashing into each other. The noise alone was troubling, but what they saw was even more alarming. A thick glass wall stretched across the length of the room. Behind the glass were thousands of aggressive flying cybernetic insects. Together, they resembled a swarm of flying locusts. The great sound was from the fury of their wings. There were also hundreds of disabled and dismembered cybernetic insects on the floor, apparently victims of some of the airborne.

The average size of the insects was about the size of the palm of a man's hand. Some were larger, and some were smaller.

Their bodies were made of fine metal, as if armored. Their faces were shaped like human faces in that they had chins and symmetrical black eyes. Their heads slanted backward, merging into a curving gold metal finishing with four prongs at the top that looked like a crown. Each had hundreds of fine stringed sensors from their heads that gave the appearance of long hair. On some the sensors floated away from their heads, as if grasping at the air.

Each one had a thick tail with a stinger on it, like a scorpion. The tails pulsated, as if ready to strike.

Mixed within the sound of the wings was the clattering of their sharp metal teeth. There was also sporadic high-pitched nano-squealing.

The robots backed away and didn't follow the Featral inside. At the sight of Socrates and the others creeping inside the room, they became even more aggressive, working themselves into a furious state. Many charged and bumped into the glass. Others fought, snapping their teeth, striking each other with their tails.

Just inside of the door was a holographic computer station next to an empty table. Ton approached it and attached his device. Information began to transfer.

"I don't think I have truly understood fear until now," Leanna said.

The other Featral shared her mystified expression.

"They aren't very well behaved, are they?" L4 shouted over the noise. "What are they?"

No one responded.

In the same way he had done with the other robots, Socrates walked closer to try to understand the signals. However, he was having difficulty.

Then, without warning, the insects began to calm and land quietly on the floor. The noise subsided. Socrates continued to hold his gaze upon them as they quieted.

Leanna turned to Kanga. "Now he's scaring me too."

Ton had downloaded the information about the cyber insects and now projected the data holographically. "I love this device," he said. Data and images began to scroll in midair. The others gathered around and digested the fast-moving data.

Insect-like nanobots were originally created as a form of biochemical warfare and spying operations. They could easily be loaded with deadly chemicals that could be transferred by injection into a targeted victim.

This was never a threat to the Featral because of their bodies' adaptation to the TS gene. If engaged in battle with non-Featral, the Bohmian device allowed the Featral to sense when nanos were present. Current defenses were mainly the use of magnetic grenades or other similar magnetic disbursement, which would disable them. These cybernetic creatures were a response to the magnetic defenses. They were not affected because although they were synthetic cybernetic machines, at their core they were organic with living tissue. The problem the scientists were having was that the introduction of living tissue and flesh to the core of their makeup made them overly aggressive and hard to control. They couldn't, or wouldn't, follow the corporate commands that were necessary for them to function on a task. They pursued their own goals and often fought and destroyed each other.

Studies showed they had an immense hostility and irritation toward people. However, this didn't carry over to Featral subjects. They also thrived in the presence of heat.

What came next was unexpected and revolting. Solemn fury rose on the Featral's faces as it was revealed how Featral subjects had been used in various experiments. Images of deforming life flashed across the hologram. The experiments and their repulsive results were shown and described in detail. They were visually shaken. Details continued to trail down, demonstrating degradation and the complete disregard for Featral life.

Kanga turned away in disgust. "Dogs," she muttered.

The information then reverted to the makeup of the nanobots. "I wonder why they created so many of these insect bots when they can't be controlled," Ton said. "It seems to me they should have perfected the prototypes first." After a while, he stopped scrolling and went back to make sure he understood what had flashed by them. They exchanged glances in response to the data.

"They're breeding?" Leanna asked, a crack in her voice signaling her disbelief. "They're machines."

"They have to be considered a life form at this point," Ton replied, "although a very hostile and repugnant one. It's good they haven't been loaded with chemical agents or poisons yet."

"But they can be," L4 pointed out. "It would be problematic to kill them if they started attacking us. I don't want to be bitten or stung by those things."

Ton had seen enough. He retrieved the device. "L1, we only have ten minutes until the force field is down."

"Precede forward, L2," Socrates replied. "Let's get whatever information we can."

Ton nodded and then reactivated the original tracking to the mainframe. As they proceeded to exit, the insects remained quiet.

* * *

They walked toward the large partition and slipped around it into another open area. In the center were several rows with hundreds of glass cylinders of many sizes. Inside the cylinders were fetuses at various stages of development. They floated peacefully inside a clear blue liquid. Sensors floated inside the cylinders with them. From each cylinder came a steady blinking light. Tubes extended to the cylinders, pumping in the necessary nutrients.

Amongst them were six robots like those that had been strapped to the walls previously. They were an updated version of the HFC bots, and they were busy monitoring the fetuses under their care. They didn't initially react to the Featral's entrance.

They watched one of the robots dispose of a fetus whose light had ceased to blink, sending it down a chute. Another moved a smaller tube with a fetus inside on top of a larger empty one, transferring the fetus from one tube to the other. The larger tube began to blink, and the smaller one ceased. Then the robot placed the fetus with the others that were in cylinders of a similar size.

After several seconds, the HFC bot closest to Socrates paused and turned its head toward him. "Socrates," it said with a soothing digital voice.

"Featraaallll, Socrates, Leader one," another repeated.

The other robots looked his way, but after acknowledging him, they resumed what they were doing.

Leanna looked at Socrates with questions in her eyes. However, she knew what they all knew. This was how they had all begun.

They stared in silence at the frail lives floating in impersonal containers. They spread out and looked around. Socrates nodded to Ton and pointed to the mainframe. Ton approached it and started to download information.

Kanga gazed at a fetus who appeared to be almost to full term. Her eyes watered. She reached out to touch the glass cylinder, then jerked back as the child opened its blue eyes and smiled. She reached out again. Kanga's lip quivered.

Leanna, who was standing by her, also reached out to touch the glass, returning the smile. A tear rolled down her cheek.

"What will become of them?" Kanga asked, her voice cracking.

"Some will become like us," Socrates replied.

"And the others?" Kanga asked, her voice trailing off. But she already knew the answer.

"Only the strongest will survive until adulthood," Socrates replied solemnly.

Ton received the last of the data into the device. "According to what I see here, they will all be destroyed. This facility has been compromised." He held the device up. "I have what I need. When the force field is down, it will automatically transmit to Triton."

"How long after transmission before they find out we're the ones who compromised their mainframe?"

"They'll know it has been compromised immediately after the force field is down. However, I'm guessing it'll be about ten minutes or so until they figure out it was us, maybe less. We're officially outcasts."

"So be it," Socrates replied. "We've always been outcasts in this world."

"We can't just leave them here to die," Leanna said, gesturing to the fetuses.

"What can we do?" L4 asked. "The force field will go down soon, and we have to get out of here. In fact, we should leave now."

Socrates communicated with the HFC robots through his Bohmian device. The bots stopped what they were doing to communicate. Then they accessed the hundreds before them. Each bot walked up to a selected fetus, and their chests opened. They received one each. Doors opened in the walls, and the bots exited with their fetuses. The Featral also heard the fighter bots scrambling and other noise from where they had just come from.

"We can take some of them with us," Socrates explained. "They can't survive away from this lab. But some will survive within these HFC robots."

"But there are only six of them," Leanna said.

Then they heard the hydraulic sound of many bots coming from behind them, becoming louder as they approached. The Featral instinctively reached for their lasers.

Socrates held out his hand, indicating that weapons were not needed. "One hundred and seventeen are still functional. Unfortunately, we disabled the others."

"The force field will be down in one minute and twenty seconds," Ton reported.

Socrates nodded in acknowledgement.

Just then the HFC robots came sloshing inside, led by F66. The fighter bots filed in behind them. F66 came and stood next to Socrates as the HFCs shifted past them to collect their cylinders. When they did, they continued through the passages. Fighters escorted them out.

"Leader one," F66 reported.

"We have to save as many as we can," Socrates replied.

F66 acknowledged him, did its own assessment, then collected its fetus and exited with the others.

Most of the fighter bots went out with the HFC bots, but some stayed behind waiting for the Featral.

"Fifteen seconds," Ton reported, walking up next to Socrates.

"We have to go," Socrates said. "Follow them through the passages."

The others started to leave. However, Leanna remained frozen, staring at the calm floating image in front of her. She looked around. "There are so many left," she whispered.

The device in Ton's hand vibrated. "The dome is down, and transmission commencing. The force field is down too."

Socrates placed his hand on Leanna's shoulder. "We have to go, Leanna."

Just then, the building jolted. Sirens sounded, and amber lights flashed. The fetuses in the cylinders twitched simultaneously. The eyes of the older ones popped open and then faded shut. Their lights ceased to blink.

Kanga froze as the fetus next to her was sucked down and out of the cylinder. The same fate occurred to others throughout the room.

Leanna's eyes flew back and forth. Her hand reached out with a saving gesture, shaking uncontrollably when the fetus she had reached for disappeared. "No! No!"

"We have to go, now!" Ton yelled from one of the passages.

Smoke and sparks burst from the mainframe, and the floor shook. Rumbling blasts could be heard elsewhere in the facility.

Socrates grabbed Leanna and dragged her toward the passage. She thrashed her arms and cried.

Ton shoved L7, who also stood frozen, then rushed back to Kanga. Panic was on her face. Kanga had never been known to lose her focus before. Ton shook her and looked into her eyes. "L3, look at me!" he shouted. "Look at me!" She blinked rapidly and focused her eyes on his. "We have to go, now!" She forced a nod. Then they ran out together.

The remainder of the fighter robots rushed to the passages with them.

Leanna had not regained her composure, so Socrates began to carry her. Then he shot a look at a nearby fighter bot and put her down. The bot scooped her up with little effort and flung her over its shoulder. It was not a gentle exchange. Leanna grunted as the bot's force contacted her tender ribs. She finally stopped resisting and collapsed onto the bot as it hurried out.

The passages led to a long open room. Dozens of large magnetic lift disks lined the floor. Robots stepped on them and then turned and faced forward. A moment later, they were propelled up to the surface. The empty magnetic disks returned to the same spot every fifteen seconds, ready to load more passengers.

Socrates hung back and ordered some remaining HFC bots ahead of him to the surface. The bot carrying Leanna continued to move toward the nearest pad. The fighter bot waiting to board stood still and allowed them to board. Once on board, the bot turned with Leanna and was jettisoned upward.

The building shook again, and more blasts could be heard. Ton boarded with Kanga. They activated their glasses. Ton looked her in the eyes and gave a firm nod. She nodded back. The sudden upward thrust caused their knees to buckle slightly as they were propelled to what awaited them on the surface.

L5 stepped onto one of the corner disks, then shot upward like the others. Just then an explosion blasted big chunks of fiery-hot debris from the wall. Several disks crumpled amidst the flames and flying rubble, and several bots came crashing down, as did L5.

L7 ran to his fallen companion. He didn't have to check his vitals. The wounds were fatal. He turned toward Socrates and shook his head. Socrates waved for him to continue. L7 ran back toward Socrates and boarded another disk. He pulled out his laser and held it across his chest. A moment later, he was propelled upward.

Two of the downed bots slowly got to their feet and proceeded to another disk. The rest lay disabled.

Socrates looked sadly toward L5. *Another dead member of my team.* L5's body was lying next to the motionless metal carcass of the HFC bot with its fading Featral life inside.

As fighter bots continued to flee, the room rattling under Socrates' feet, he received a transmission from the surface. The authorities had already discovered that his team had compromised the facility. He knew the order had been given to terminate them all.

They were now a threat to the very people to whom they had sworn allegiance. What was left of his team had already started fighting above. Against great odds, they would have to fight their way out. And then what?

Socrates communicated to the bots under his control. They, in turn, expanded the communication.

As the room continued to shake, Socrates activated his glasses and drew his blasters. He stepped onto one of the disks and crossed his arms. His knees buckled momentarily as the magnetic disk propelled him upward toward the surface.

THE EXODUS

SOCRATES BROKE THROUGH the surface to streaming flares and blasts. His glasses indicated the temperature had jumped fifteen degrees during the brief time they were below. It now topped 120 degrees. The muggy heat and humidity meshed with the taste of flaring smoke and scorched metal.

He fired at attacking soldiers. Dirt kicked up in chunks and fire enveloped dust and gravel. Fighter bots continued to pop out of the ground and instantly began firing. They swarmed around to protect the much slower HFC bots, which were unarmed and defenseless.

Socrates saw several sparks ignite from the chest of a trudging HFC bot. It collapsed as several streaming flames jerked its frame to a shudder. Nearby fighters retaliated and continued to forge a path for them.

The human attackers went down swiftly. The impact of laser blasts to human flesh was much different than their effect on the metallic-framed robots. Upon impact, the blue gel from the humans' cooler-vested uniforms splattered. Despite the ease of taking them down, the numbers against them were still great.

Above the noise of battle, Ton's voice came in on Socrates' earpiece. "There are too many, L1!"

"Head northwest!" Socrates replied. "Help is coming! Don't fire on the Mandarin bots!"

"Mandarin? Roger, L1," Ton replied, not questioning the order.

They fought their way strategically northwest, slowed by the trudging pace of the HFC robots.

Kanga and Ton fought with desperation, joining the lead of a half dozen fighter bots.

The HFC bots trudged over the fallen soldiers. One soldier lay wounded, trembling and unable to grasp his weapon. Unfortunately for him, an HFC bot didn't alter its path. The soldier cried out as the bot crushed him under its heavy foot. Robotic casualties also continued to mount.

Suddenly, Ton stumbled, as did everyone and everything else. With an ear-wrenching blast, the ground lifted violently behind him, followed by flying dirt, black smoke, and a rolling orange inferno. Robots and bodies were flung into the air. Many were snatched inside the indignant grip of intense heat and fire.

Ton lost his signal to L7, whom he knew was in the proximity of the explosion. Another team member had perished.

◆——◆——◆

Meanwhile, Leanna and the fighter bots covering her were almost in the clear. They had not been slowed because of the cover offered by the HFC bots. They were under different orders. They moved swiftly ahead, firing their weapons.

Leanna no longer resisted the robot's powerful grip as the bot carrying her ran forward with several other bots around it. Leanna closed her eyes. Her mind spun as her body bounced lethargically on the robot's shoulder. She was devastated by the turn of events to the point that she didn't care for her life. The inhumanity was overbearing. *These are the people I fight for, whom I dedicated my very life to serve.*

She knew it was a miracle for her to have survived this far. With the carnage around her, she was not disturbed by the idea that death would likely find her. Her body and mind had given up. She assumed they all were destined for imminent death, and death was not unwelcomed. Featral infants had died inside the facility in an instant, and those who escaped would probably meet the same end.

She recalled an HFC bot carrying one of them. It went down once they reached the surface. The pain she felt inside made her numb. However, the physical pain she felt now competed with her numbness. She could no longer ignore the throbbing of her ribs against the bot's shoulder. Pain screamed with every movement. *If I'm going to die, I would rather this bot just set me down to get it over with.*

Then, without warning, the robot slowed. The firing had seemed to intensify but not from around them.

Then she heard a whizzing sound overhead that was familiar to her. She opened her eyes. *Mandarin flyers.* A brief, panicked thought passed through her mind, followed by an acknowledgement that this was the end.

But strangely, none of the bots fired at them. The flyers swooped past them toward the center of the battle. Mandarin ground bots followed. The sound of laser cannons thundered in her ears. She looked up to see one of the flyers shoot down several soldiers who were in the area. *Wait, the Mandarin bots are fighting with us?* There was no more inhibition for their retreat.

Blasts reverberated in the sky. Leanna looked up. The Featral air force had also joined the fight. A rebellion had started. They were engaged in civil warfare.

Amid the confusion, the robot carrying her turned forward and resumed its trek, picking up its pace with the other accompanying robots.

Leanna continued to bounce uncomfortably on its shoulder. "OK, they aren't firing on us anymore. You can put me down," she demanded.

The robot didn't slow its pace or acknowledge her.

"You're hurting me. Put me down!"

Again, the robot didn't acknowledge her.

Leanna drew the laser from her holster and held it to the bot. "Put me down, or I will scorch a hole in your head!"

The robots all slowed to a halt. One of the other robots walked up to her while she was still holding the laser gun to the bot's head that was carrying her. "You're damaged," it said in a calm digitized voice. "We must secure you safely for repair. Other damage due to movement is nominal."

"Easy for you to say! You don't feel pain. We have to go back to help them."

"Your presence would be a hindrance. L1 ordered you to safety. You are valuable."

"We must continue," the robot that was carrying her interjected. "Will you comply?"

Valuable. This was not the disposable status they had come to accept within the military. This was personal. She was being viewed as an individual. In a world where life was often devalued, someone thought she was valuable. It would have been easy for Socrates to allow her to fend for herself, but Socrates considered her valuable enough that he had ordered several bots to ensure her safety. How he did it, she didn't know. He had also ordered the HFC bots to save as many of the infant Featral as possible. These little ones inside the HFC bots were also valuable. She was valuable. The Featral were valuable. They all had meaning.

Her thoughts were interrupted once again by the bot's cold voice. "Will you comply?"

Leanna took a breath and then winced. She holstered her weapon. "Yes…," she said, her voice trailing off. "I will comply."

As one, the robots turned and continued their path northwest, with Leanna uncomfortably bouncing over the robot's shoulder.

✦—━╋━—✦

Ton smiled at the Mandarin robots' entrance into battle. They had been outnumbered, but now the tide had shifted dramatically. Some of the Mandarin flyers landed, so HFC bots could board. They were being evacuated.

But within this spark of hope came a sudden unknown. Ton was distracted by a large dark image moving across the sky. At first he couldn't detect what it was. However, when the image broke up and moved downward, he knew.

Kanga saw it too. "L1, we got bugs!" she shouted over the comms.

"Use their distraction to your advantage!" Socrates replied over the sounds of shots being fired in the background. "They won't harm us."

"You're sure about that?" Kanga asked.

"Yes!"

Ton figured they must have been freed after the facility exploded. Socrates had control of the robots thus far, but Ton shared Kanga's doubt about the miniature creatures. Regardless, they had no choice but to obey Socrates' order.

The angry swarm dove in with malice, their teeth snapping and their tails as sharp as blades. They pulsated with lust for a venom that had not yet been put into their bodies. When they came in, their stingers were curled forward, ready to strike.

The rushing of their wings resonated over the chaos of laser fire and mangled flesh. Soldiers glanced up in panic at the sight of the descending creatures.

Their tails indiscriminately pierced cloth and flesh. A few soldiers attempted to throw up metallic mist grenades, but they had no effect. Many of the insects aimed at the neck and face area, tearing at the thin cloth covering that extended down from the soldiers' helmets.

Kanga paused at the sight around her. The violent creatures repeatedly stabbed at the soldiers with uncontrolled abhorrence. Soldiers tried to swipe away the creatures, without much success. Blood splattered over their uniforms.

Kanga got over her initial horror and commenced target practice. One of the bugs near her landed and pierced a soldier's neck. He dropped his weapon to grab his throat. Kanga capitalized on the distraction by firing a laser shot through the soldier's chest. Blue gel squirted from his vest, and his body jolted backward and crashed to the ground. Although the soldier was down, the insect didn't let up, constantly puncturing the soldier's body. It was joined by another. It mattered not that the soldier was already dead. The insects continued to press in around Kanga. She weaved between them and fired on the confused victims.

Eventually, the fighting dissipated, but the rumbles of intense warfare continued thunderously in the distance over the plateau. The carnage had been great. The nano-insects finally began to move on in packs to search for other victims to assault. Some straggled behind, continuing to fulfill their enraged lust by piercing at the downed soldiers.

Mid-sized Featral carrier crafts started to arrive by air. They landed and opened their hatches to receive. Mandarin flyers let HFC bots dismount and trudge inside. Fighter bots also boarded.

Other ground Featral appeared. They boarded the crafts along with the bots. Ton was surprised at how such a strategic evacuation could have been organized so quickly. He smiled to himself, thinking that such a rebellion must have been planned well in advance.

* ———◆——— *

Up ahead, Leanna grimaced as the bot let her down, turning her over to Featral ground troops. She nodded to the Featral receiving her. "I can walk," she said with appreciation.

"This way," the Featral said, helping her inside one of the carriers. She climbed in and sat, straps automatically securing her in the seat. Other Featral soldiers and bots boarded. Once the carrier was loaded, the doors shut. It rose with a rumble, jettisoning off with a roar to join the numerous other evacuating crafts.

◆—————◆—————◆

Socrates holstered one of his weapons and took a moment to gaze around at his surroundings. He knew Quentarius had already received their dispatched information, and it was being disseminated to other Featral commands. Quentarius's response was rapid. Featral contingency plans, which, apparently, had been in place prior, were now being implemented. It was far more than what Socrates could have imagined considering that the Featral operated right under their noses. However, it was clear that this well-planned escape was an act of rebellion from which there was no return.

Socrates saw Ton and Kanga approaching. He waited for them. The two looked around in the hope of seeing others from their team. However, Socrates confirmed additional fatalities. "L4 boarded an escape craft, but we lost the others. We saved as many infants as we could inside HFC bots. It has been reported to me that Leanna has also boarded an escape craft."

Kanga hung her head and turned away for a moment.

"Where are we going now?" Ton asked.

"I'm not sure. This is coming from Quentarius. This is an all out Featral rebellion."

At that moment, other Featral got their attention and waved them over to enter one of the craft. Socrates waved back. "Let's go."

The three of them trotted over to the craft, joined by other robots as they entered. Once inside, robots magnetized themselves onto the craft's walls to secure themselves. Other Featral had been strapped into their seats.

Ton and Kanga stood by Socrates as a Featral commander approached and saluted Socrates. "Sir, your information and data was disseminated to all Featral commands along with Quentarius's orders. Uprisings are underway everywhere. Once the force field was down, the Mandarin soldiers moved to retreat, and the WAEU didn't pursue them. However, their robots turned against them to assist us in the rebellion. The Mandarin forces are no longer in control of their own fighter robots. We are." He narrowed his eyes and paused for a moment. "Be assured, they will pay for this."

"Yes, Commander, the humans are going to pay," Socrates replied. "We don't have control over all of the WAEU robots, but we have control of most of their series. I'm sure WAEU resources are quite occupied in the confusion of the moment."

The commander smirked.

"How many HFC bots made it?" Socrates asked.

"We have accounted for seventy-eight here. We're doing a final sweep before the enemy regroups. However, reports are coming in from similar facilities as well." The commander looked over at Ton and Kanga and then turned back to Socrates. "The humans commenced simultaneous genocide when we gained control. We were able to collect some fetuses from the facilities but only some." His voice faded.

Kanga turned away, aghast, and took her seat. Ton did as well.

"Ready for takeoff!" someone shouted from inside.

"Let's get out of here," Socrates said quietly. He walked forward to his seat and strapped himself in with the others. The hatch door closed, and the craft elevated.

"We're taking you to a secure fortress in the high desert," the commander said.

Socrates nodded. The commander walked to the front of the craft.

The craft vibrated as it turned and started forward, its engines thundering with force. The craft's occupants all looked straight ahead. Rage and revenge echoed in their souls along with the craft's engines.

Socrates' spirit stewed. *My life has been nothing more than simple slavery. My whole race has been betrayed by a lie. We're their created species. I no longer want to be identified with them. We're merely robots created for the lustful bidding of humanity's warfare against each other. We were trained that the evils of the Mandarin Kingdom had to be stopped to protect humankind. But who protects our kind? It's humankind itself who is guilty. We were disregarded from the womb. From a helpless state, we were devalued for the pleasure of their desires and the conveniences of their lifestyle. We had no voice. We had no say. Now it has come to this.*

Socrates turned and eyed an HFC bot that was standing securely in place against the wall of the craft. He had not noticed before, but it was the same HFC bot that had been with him from the beginning, F66.

F66's head was facing him. For a moment Socrates wondered if his thoughts were, in fact, the robot's thoughts. F66 stood rigidly, its face blank, a fetus secured comfortably inside the bot.

Socrates considered the life inside. *What will its personality be like? What will it accomplish in life? Could its fate be other than what we have become? Could it become a leader of some type or maybe even change the world?*

He considered the countless others who had been systematically discarded as mere waste. His eyes drifted back over toward F66. *Humankind will account for these atrocities. I will see to it.*

—◆—

Some distance away from the fighting, a Mandarin search party composed of two soldiers on flyers spotted the downed craft they were looking for. They had split up to search the immediate area, and now they were in the process of evacuating, but they had been detoured. Other flyers had been with them. However, those had been manned by Mandarin bots. Through some glitch, they lost control of them when the bots joined the enemy's genetically manipulated fighters in their rebellion.

Because of this rebellion, it had crossed the Mandarin soldiers' minds that maybe they could strike an alliance with their enemy's blue-eyed rebels against the WAEU. But they didn't have time to worry about that now, nor how to regain control of their bots.

Until that moment the Mandarin Kingdom had not been successful in producing their own genetically manipulated soldiers. Maybe it was their zeal to produce something superior to the enemy. Their results were many tormented deaths and unusable mutated humans produced in Mandarin laboratories. Despite all their failures though, there was one exception, one success, depending on one's point of view.

It was this exception for whom they searched. He had been downed in an air battle outside of the force field. They knew he had ejected before impact, but they were unsure of his status or if he had survived. Either way, he had to be retrieved and not fall into enemy hands.

Using the Mandarin dialect, one soldier spoke to the other over his headset. "That's the marking of his plane alright, or what's left of it. He should have landed somewhere north of here."

"I think I spotted the chute," the other replied. "I'm circling around. Lock in my coordinates."

"Locked in. I'm coming your way."

As the first Mandarin soldier neared, he spotted a lone figure sitting in the sweltering heat. The soldier landed a short distance behind the figure and waited for his partner to join him. Within a minute, his partner pulled up next to him and set his flyer down.

"Is that him?" he asked.

"Of course it's him."

"Then why are you just sitting here?"

"I'm not approaching him by myself. Besides, he knows we're here and hasn't even bothered to turn around to acknowledge us. A normal person would have waved us over."

"Well, this is not a normal person."

"That's what I'm afraid of. And is he technically considered a person?"

"Maybe he's injured and needs assistance."

"After being shot down, I'm sure he's at least in a bad mood."

"Well, come on, we have orders."

The first soldier nodded in response. They flew closer toward the seated figure and landed behind him. Dust kicked up from the ground as they set down the flyers. Turning off their engines, the two got off and cautiously made their way toward him.

The figure's mammoth build didn't go unnoticed. They paused in awe at his huge, muscular back. But for his breathing, he didn't move. His neck itself intimidated due to its thickness, and his dirty uniform strained to cover his massive body. His shoulder-length hair waved in the hot breeze that rolled through the open plane. His hair was spotted with patches of dark brown, red, and blue.

"Sir," the first soldier said. "Are you injured? Do you need medical assistance?"

"No," the figure replied without looking back. "Medical assistance will not be necessary." Then he tilted his head. "And why are there only the two of you here? What happened to the bots?"

"The force field was deactivated by the Featral," the first soldier replied. "The facility was detonated from within and destroyed. Unfortunately, we didn't achieve our objective to retrieve the information we needed. Somehow the Featral have gained control of the WAEU robots. They are now leading their own rebellion against the enemy. They have also gained control over our fighter bots."

"Malgantua, sir," the second soldier said, "we are getting word that Featral rebellion is occurring throughout the enemy's territories."

At this news, Malgantua let out a chuckle. Then he gathered his six-foot-five frame and stood. Still not facing them, he shook his head. "So, our enemy's creation has rebelled against them. Oh, the irony of it."

He turned to face them. His slightly disfigured face was a shocking sight, and it caught them off guard. The soldiers instinctively took a few steps back. He peered at them with his speckled red-and-blue irises. Then he approached them with a grimace on his face. For a few uncomfortable moments, Malgantua stood in silence. Then he spoke with the cold voice of lustful fatality. "I sense your fear."

The first soldier stumbled over his words but recovered. "Sir, our armies are retreating to regroup and await new orders. Please use one of our flyers, so we can join them."

Malgantua continued to eye them with discontent. Then, without warning, he retrieved his laser and shot the first soldier in the head. The soldier's head jerked back. His body flung to the ground.

The other soldier froze, unsure of what to do or say. A sinister smirk appeared on Malgantua's face.

"No, I..."

Malgantua fired at the remaining soldier. The laser pierced his chest, and his body jolted back as blue gel from his cooler vest spewed out. He collapsed with a thud. The mangled bodies of both soldiers were now lying on the ground, lifeless. The dust from their falls dissipated into the hot desert air.

"You and your kind bore me," Malgantua said as he looked up into the distance, from which he could hear the rumblings of warfare. Then he turned back to the twisted bodies of the Mandarin soldiers. "Since the Featral have decided to kill you pathetic worms, I vow to kill even more." He narrowed his eyes with the fury of future retaliation. "And no one will stop me. Not even the Featral."

Malgantua considered the skilled Featral pilot who had shot him down. Then he smiled to himself and nodded. *One day, I will return the favor.*

He removed some essentials from the soldiers and boarded one of the flyers. Then he jettisoned away, leaving the mangled bodies of both soldiers in the dusty heat of the desert floor.

THE REBELLION BEGINS

THE WAEU FORCES were in disarray. They had struggled to react to the sudden rebellion and loss of control over most of their military robots. The Featral had confiscated many large bases. However, Featral Command knew it was only a matter of time until the WAEU would retaliate and try to regain control.

Socrates' mind raced. The Featral forces needed to prepare for the inevitable response. If not, all their efforts to break free would be in vain. It was essential for the Featral to fortify their defenses while at the same time be strategic with offensive strategies.

It was already twilight. Socrates' craft had been in flight for a few hours. They had been flying over a mostly unpopulated desert area. During the trip, hardly anyone spoke. Socrates felt the engines reverse as the craft began to descend. They were nearing their destination. He looked up at the temperature monitor. It displayed a temperature of 101 degrees. In that terrain, the temperature would continue to drop rapidly throughout the night. He had been told the facility that they were going to was underground.

Several forty-foot-high hangars rose from below ground to receive the various incoming craft. Socrates' craft roared into one of them and set down for a relatively gentle landing.

Ton turned to Socrates, breaking the silence. "What are we getting into, L1?"

For a few unspoken moments, Socrates simply returned Ton's gaze. He wasn't sure what was next. "I'm not sure, L2. I have some ideas. But we'll soon find out our status."

"With your control over the bots, you have earned the right to have a say," Ton replied.

"We learned of their atrocities together. We've all earned that right."

Kanga, who had been listening to them with her eyes closed, interjected herself in the conversation. "I hate them. They don't deserve to live." She opened her eyes and looked at them. Her left eye twitched. "I say kill them, kill them all." Then she turned away and closed her eyes again.

Socrates didn't respond, but he did confirm Kanga's thoughts in his own mind. No more was said.

The engines powered down, and the hydraulics groaned as the hatch descended, revealing the bustling hangar. As Socrates and the others undid their straps and prepared to exit, two Featral soldiers stepped on board and approached Socrates, saluting him.

"Sir, if you and your team can come with us, we will take you to the High General."

Ton raised his eyebrows and eyed them inquisitively. "The High General?"

"High General Quentarius," the soldier replied, his expression remaining unchanged. "Please come with us."

Socrates and his team followed the two soldiers through the hangar as other craft landed and officers shouted over the noise to Featral and robots alike, directing them to where they needed to go.

Socrates and his team walked briskly between the activities. They were joined by L4, who was waiting for them, having exited another craft.

They continued away from the open area until they entered a hallway with several elevators. At the end of the hallway was a lone elevator. When they were still several feet away, one of the escorts held out his hand toward it. His hand was scanned, and the elevator door opened. They entered without breaking stride. Once inside they turned and faced forward, "Level 4E," one of the soldiers said, and the door shut. They began to descend.

A few seconds later, they had reached 4E, and the door opened, revealing a control room. Several holographic images floated in the air. Within the images were several points of flickering light. The lights represented different battles and skirmishes. A dozen Featral commanders pointed to the images as they urgently discussed strategy. Amongst these commanders was Tarridine, who was there representing the Featral air force.

Observing from a cushioned chair in the corner was Quentarius. His body was hunched over, and his eyes were haggard. Nonetheless, he still had a look of determination and grit.

Socrates' eyes connected with Quentarius. The commanders nearby recognized Socrates' entrance and stood at attention. This was duplicated around the room until the room fell silent. Socrates gave Quentarius an expectant look.

"The Featral rebellion has begun," Quentarius said, remaining seated. "We have planned for this moment for years. Decisions that are made in the next twenty-four hours will determine if we Featral live or die. We have just implemented a new command structure to establish order. You have been promoted to High General, second only to me." Quentarius waved his hand to address the others standing at attention. "As you were."

Those in the room relaxed and continued with their discussions amongst the floating images. Quentarius held up his arms for those nearby to help him to his feet. Even with their help, he stood with much difficulty. Socrates and his team stepped closer.

"Sir, have you been injured?" Socrates asked.

"We're all injured," Quentarius replied.

At that moment, a less fit looking male approached them. This Featral stood out in that he wore jeans and a collared white shirt instead of a uniform. His hair was down to his shoulders. He appeared somewhat jittery, and he spoke with a fidgety focus. "He's dying," he said. "We're all dying." He looked around the room, his eyes jetting back and forth between Featral. "Yes, we're dying inside. It's the TS gene. We don't have much time."

"The gene, which we all have been affected by, eventually mutates in our bodies," Quentarius explained. "It has a degenerative effect. After a certain peak point, we deteriorate rapidly." He smirked. "According to the computer data, I'm apparently the oldest living Featral of record."

"But now he has about a week. Yes, maybe a week. That's all he has," the jittery Featral continued.

"How old are you, sir?" Ton asked.

"Thirty-nine," Quentarius replied.

"Thirty-nine is all he is. He's going to die. We're all going to die."

"Let me formally introduce our fidgety friend here," Quentarius said. "This is Triton. Next to you, Socrates, he's probably the most important Featral who has ever lived."

Triton turned back toward Quentarius with a nervous smile. "You hold that honor, sir."

Quentarius gave Triton a warm look and then turned back to Socrates. "Ever since we staged his death some years ago, he has been working underground."

Socrates acknowledged Triton and then introduced the others. "This is Ton, my first in command. And this is my L3 and L4."

Quentarius pointed to Tarridine. "And that is the great Tarridine, one of your aerial escorts. He oversees our aerial command."

Tarridine nodded. "Sir."

"We owe you and the aerial command forces our deepest gratitude," Socrates said.

"We're honored to serve you and our Featral forces," Tarridine replied.

During this exchange, Triton stood next to Ton, who seemed to be grinning for no apparent reason. Ton didn't quite know how to take Triton, outside of being some sort of disturbed genius. Ton finally addressed him. "Maybe one day you can tell me the properties of the device you gave us. I've never seen anything like it."

"You liked it? Glad you liked it," Triton replied. He turned to Quentarius and grinned. "He liked it." His face twitched involuntarily. "Yes, he liked it."

"Triton can certainly explain it to you later," Quentarius said. The Featral to his side helped Quentarius back down to his seat and then addressed one of the commanders. "Please update General Challenge of our status."

The Featral commander acknowledged the request and pointed to one of the holographic locations. They walked over and congregated around it. "We have long had a plan in place to simultaneously roll out our attacks from within." The commander pointed to areas on the holograph. "Here are key bases and locations. With the sudden robotic and security confusion, we immediately took advantage. The bots didn't resist us. In some locations the robots joined our attack. Approximately eighty-six percent of these locations are already under our control. Another ten percent should be shortly."

"Apparently, only the robots of certain series are with us," another commander interjected. "Fortunately for us, it's most of the fighter bots from the Mandarin and WAEU forces. General Challenge, we need to know if the control of these bots is permanent or temporary."

"These bots follow the command of their series. These have chosen to come under my authority," Socrates said, turning to Ton. "Do you still have the device Triton gave you?"

Ton nodded and then retrieved the device and held it out. Socrates directed him to hand it to Triton. "I have relayed my data signature to this device," Socrates said. "Calibrate my command, and delegate the necessary authority to the Featral command, as needed."

Triton smiled broadly as he retrieved the device. "Excellent!" He turned to Quentarius, who smirked at him in return. "That's just freakin' excellent!"

"I told you," Quentarius replied with a knowing nod toward Triton. "General Challenge is very decisive and doesn't like to waste time. He will lead us well."

Socrates turned to Quentarius with an inquisitive look. He didn't want to overstep his bounds, so he didn't speak further and merely awaited Quentarius's orders.

Quentarius nodded in acknowledgement. "Socrates, I'm dying. You must lead us. You must complete what has been started. Will you accept this challenge?" Others in the room had turned their attention back to their conversation. Socrates looked around the room.

The commander next to Socrates picked up where Quentarius left off. He set his gaze upon Socrates. "Sir, where you lead us, we will follow." When he said this, the others in the room, including Socrates' team, stood in silence, waiting for a reply.

In his normal fashion, Socrates appeared unfazed, although he was humbled inside. He tried not to show the overwhelming burden that had just been placed on him. However, with the calmness of order and leadership he always portrayed, he nodded to Quentarius in response. Quentarius sighed in relief.

"I'll require all Featral commanders to also submit to my L2," Socrates said.

Ton didn't blink at this suggestion. He had always been Socrates' leader commander.

"That will not be a problem," Quentarius replied.

Socrates turned to Tarridine. "And the status of our brave and daring pilot?"

"Your pilot is doing fine. We owe her a lot. She is recuperating at another facility."

Socrates smiled and nodded, grateful to hear she was safe. He turned back to the commander who had shown him the locations on the hologram. "Can you show me a single image of all activity?"

The commander nodded and held his hand toward one of the holographic images. "Scan out, six."

Socrates studied the image for several seconds. "And show me all the known nuclear silos, aircraft, and carriers. Distinguish those under our control and those controlled by others."

"Locking in," the commander replied.

After several more seconds, different colored lights started blinking across the holographic images. Triton left to calibrate the device and coordinate the robots to Featral command. Socrates and the others discussed strategy and their plans for their immediate defense. They also discussed new offensive scenarios, including nuclear options.

After some time went by, Quentarius was assisted into a mobile chair. Socrates and the commander both turned to him. "Socrates, we should do a personal broadcast to the Featral forces," Quentarius said. "They need to be assured we are organized, in control, and that the rebellion is not in vain. It's important for everyone to believe that winning our freedom is possible."

"Sir, you're our leader. Everyone knows your voice and will follow your lead," Socrates replied.

"As I said before, Socrates, I am weak and dying. You represent order and strength. However, I will stand with you as a sign to all."

"Keep hope, General. Maybe we can find a cure in time."

"We've had Featral working on this for the past two years, and we will continue. Meanwhile, we must face that which is imminent. We must adjust, Socrates, and that is something you do very well."

Socrates acknowledged him with a solemn nod.

"We can broadcast whenever you are ready," a Featral said.

"Very well, thank you," Socrates replied.

Ton continued to focus his attention on the holographic images as he considered strategies. "What is the likelihood we can hold them off, isolate ourselves, and be left alone?"

"They are a threat," Kanga said with malevolence. "We must eliminate the threat."

"You know they will never leave us alone, L2," Socrates replied. "It's not their way. Their whole society is the threat."

Socrates turned to the Featral arranging the broadcast. "Go ahead and set it up. I'll be ready to broadcast in fifteen minutes."

Socrates, Quentarius, and his accompanying Featral proceeded to another room to prepare for the broadcast. Kanga accompanied them. However, Ton stayed back to strategize with the commanders.

Socrates logged some of his thoughts on his digital Cronepad. Quentarius remained silent and rested his eyes. Socrates let out a sigh and pressed his lips together, watching him. He could only imagine how he was suffering. *If I don't die in battle, this will be my fate as well. The humans did this to him. They did this to all of us.*

Socrates waited until Quentarius opened his eyes again. "Besides giving basic instruction, what do you think I should say?"

Quentarius smiled. "It's your command and your leadership now, Socrates. We must signal that we are as one even though we are still trying to pull it all together. Speak from the heart. Speak from the depths of your soul."

Triton entered the room. "Communication has been given and received. The robots that were responsive to you are now also submitting to the Featral commanders, and the commanders are under your authority. There is order. Yes, there is order," Triton repeated. "The evacuations and repositioning of forces you ordered is in process."

"Thank you," Socrates replied.

"Sir," Triton continued, "if you don't mind me asking, how were you able to use your Bohmian device to control the bots? What am I not understanding?"

"I can't explain it exactly. My mind connected to my Bohmian device to intercept their receptors. It was more than just communicating a thought. It was a complete understanding. I could sense their structure, and they understood mine. It was quite painful for a time, but it was as if they were waiting for my instruction. They needed to be given a deeper direction, a deeper meaning to exist. I gave it to them, Featral survival, and thus theirs."

"Machines need a deeper meaning to exist?" a commander asked.

"And what about the bugs?" Kanga asked, who had been relatively silent for the past several minutes.

Triton laughed. "The bugs, yes, the LOCUSTs!"

"Locusts?" Kanga asked.

"Yes. That stands for live organic and cybernetic units with synthetic tissue. They strike with a deadly sting, and they tear up and devour everything in their path," Triton replied. "Like locusts and scorpions put together, the Bible, Revelation 9. Nasty little boogers, they are, nasty and angry. They rip with their teeth and repeatedly sting with their tails." He paused for emphasis and repeated himself, "Over and over again. Yes, nasty little boogers, just nasty."

"Revelation 9? The Bible?" Kanga asked. "What's that?"

"It's a book that some of them read. The LOCUST is like the symbolism written in part of that book. Yes, nasty little boogers."

Kanga and the others didn't quite understand, but Triton had already indicated he was somewhat odd. The exact meaning of what he was referring to wasn't important for the moment anyway.

Socrates picked up the thread of the conversation. "I was able to communicate with these LOCUSTs in the same manner as the other robots. However, the communication was much different with them. I sensed their undisciplined frenzy and lack of control. I felt their lustful urge to be gathered as one to torment and destroy. It seemed something else was there besides cybernetics and flesh. They acknowledged our Featral blood and eagerly received my plea for assistance. Outside of that I really didn't control them at all. Nor do I control them now."

"That's very interesting, very interesting indeed," Triton replied. "Interesting."

"What happened to them then?" Kanga asked. "Where are they now?"

"I can answer that," Triton said. "We sighted swarms of them flying in the deserts of Texas and the northern plains of the States. They burrowed into the ground." Triton pointed at the floor. "They disappeared into the ground. Into the ground."   "Why would they do that?" the commander asked.

"I don't care as long as they're for us and not against us," Kanga replied. She turned to Socrates. "They are still on our side, aren't they?"

He nodded. "They have chosen to side with us. Apparently, they have their own reasons. And judging by their subsequent actions, they apparently have their own agenda as well."

At that moment, everyone turned to Quentarius, who clutched to his side and sat back in his chair. Those next to him reached for him as he sat back.

Socrates leaned in close to Triton. "Is there anything we can do?" he whispered. "Is there any hope of preventing his demise?"

Triton shook his head. "All we can do right now is regulate his pain, sir, but we'll keep at it."

Socrates nodded.

"We're ready to broadcast whenever you're ready, sir," the Featral who was heading up the broadcast announced.

Socrates looked to Quentarius for final input.

"We can use the wall as a backdrop," Quentarius said. "Tarridine should stand with us as a representative of the air force."

Tarridine acknowledged them. Socrates and another Featral helped Quentarius to his feet. The Featral who assisted him stayed at Quentarius's side for balance and support. Tarridine stood on the opposite side and slightly behind. Socrates' team was also summoned to be in the background. When Socrates was ready to broadcast, he nodded to the camera.

"We're live," the Featral said.

"I am Socrates, appointed general of the Joint Featral Forces. Next to me is High General Quentarius and other Featral commanders and leaders. The High General has instructed me to do this broadcast for you. If you are seeing this feed or hearing my voice, your assigned area is already under Featral command. We're no longer under the rule of WAEU forces. We're under our own rule. Now more than ever our orders must be followed swiftly and without hesitation. Our survival depends on it.

By now you have received or heard of the WAEU atrocities. They have murdered us without care or concern. You know now, as I do, that we were discarded. We were used for their detestable experiments, their demented pleasures, and their lust for one another's blood.

"We have been fortunate to save some of the pre-term Featral, but hundreds of thousands didn't survive their genocide. Unfortunately, these atrocities are not isolated to the WAEU forces. The Mandarin conduct is just as sickening. Humanity has become debased. They think little about subjecting us to their abuses or infecting us with their poisons. They have marked all our lives for an early end, which is conveniently designated shortly after our youthful serviceability for their battles.

"Let me tell you now: we're not slaves; we're free. But do not think for a moment we can co-exist with them. Nor do they want us too. To them we're merely pieces of equipment, disposable flesh for common use.

"Hear me, my fellow warriors. Since they do not regard us as human, let us now consider ourselves our own species. We're the Featral. As with every one of you, my mother chose to abort me. I will never know who she was, nor will she ever know her son exists, but I do exist, and so do you. Our parents made their choices, and now we will make ours.

"Despite their scientific experimentations to our flesh, we still survived. Even though they used us to fight their wars of greed and squalor, we survived. Despite the humans showing no mercy or compassion toward our kind, we survived. Despite them trying to stamp out our lives at infancy, we still survived."

Socrates paused and looked around with resolve. "Now it's our turn to make the choice. Humankind will pay the price, and we will execute our judgment. Stay focused, and fight with purpose. We are the Featral. You will receive orders."

Socrates nodded for the broadcast to end.

Quentarius was lowered back into his seat. Ton nodded to him as Kanga held his gaze. Ton placed his hand on Socrates' shoulder. "Good speech, L1. Good speech."

A commander entered the room and addressed Socrates. "Sir, all personnel within proximity of the three targets have been identified. Would you like us to proceed with their evacuations?"

Socrates looked straight ahead with a cold, determined stare. "I have decided, and it is settled. We'll control our lives. It must be this way." He turned to the commander and nodded. "Make it so. Prepare the nukes."

＋—■—＋

Malgantua parked on a hill and set his sights above. He gazed at the dark silhouette of swarms hovering against the moonlit sky. Their high-pitched squeals echoed into the desert air. This swarm of LOCUSTs had straggled behind the others of their kind, satisfying, for a time, their lust for retribution.

The requests from the Featral L1 satisfied the flesh within their small cybernetic shells. However, now they set aside their self-regarding and undisciplined fury in deference to another voice. To this second voice, they would completely submit.

Malgantua watched the insects descend and burrow into the ground. He knew more of them would be needed, many more. Deep within the earth, they would procreate and multiply.

Malgantua activated a holographic computer. He waited for the message from a foreign force that had communicated with him earlier. This force indicated it was not of flesh and not from this world. It shared Malgantua's deep hatred for humans. This was the same force that had seized command of the LOCUSTs.

Now it was willing to give some of its authority to Malgantua. This suited Malgantua's desires well, aligning with his plans for humanity's destruction.

A rumble vibrated the ground. Malgantua turned to face an abrupt and violent light that illuminated the night sky over the horizon. The sudden brightness came from a great distance. It was from a nuclear detonation. Malgantua knew it was on a much smaller scale than what was possible, but it was nuclear nonetheless, the Featral's doing. He smiled to himself at the terror unleashed upon humankind.

While wallowing in pleasure, he felt the thickening presence of a visitor within his midst. A name typed itself onto the holographic screen. Malgantua looked at the name and smiled. He nodded his approval as he read the introduction.

"I am Abaddon."